BLIGHT

Fall 2014

DIGEST

Edited by

Ron Earl Phillips
Bracken MacLeod
Jan Kozlowski

One Eye Press • Blight Digest

Blight Digest (Fall 2014)
Copyright © 2014 One Eye Press LLC

Cover art, "Venus in Red" © 2014 Dyer Wilk

"Cobwebs" © 2007 Kealan Patrick Burke.
Original published: Postscripts Magazine
Issue 11 (Summer 2007)

ISBN-13: 978-0692321164
www.OneEyePress.com
www.BlightDigest.com

TABLE OF CONTENTS

FROM THE EDITOR

Imagine if you will, a young, toe-headed boy huddled beneath his captain's bed, sitting behind its built in draws and shelves, hidden to anyone who came into the room. His bed would appear empty, and the moonlight flows in as the wind flutters the curtains of the open dormer window. He is not gone, but he is far, far away nonetheless, escaping into the pages of books and comics.

My first introduction to horror fiction came in a collection of horror stories, *Alfred Hitchcock's Ghostly Gallery*, in 1977, under that very bed. It would pale in comparison to what horror would have in store for me in the years come. But it was a foundation, the start of my own exploration of all those things that go bump in the night.

For me, it was always the idea of what lay beyond the periphery, what I couldn't see and what I couldn't control. That sense that something is there when it is not. That chill you get, and when the hair on your neck rises. That fear, a fear that you took with you to bed.

When I proposed the idea of BLIGHT DIGEST to my editors, Bracken and Jan, I wanted to capture the kind of fear you took to bed. And if not fear, then stories that kept you thinking long after the lights went out.

Through the tremendous efforts of Bracken and Jan, who read

dozens of submissions and worked together to select these first stories, and all those who submitted, I am very proud to present you this first issue of BLIGHT DIGEST.

Turn out the lights, if you must...

Ron Earl Phillips, *Publisher*
October 27, 2014

COBWEBS

by Kealan Patrick Burke

1

I began to be forgotten on a dawn no different than any other I'd seen during the past few years of my incarceration at Spring Grace Retirement Home. The ever-present burning ache in my bones was no better or worse. The sheets were still too tight, the pillow too lumpy, the room a little too cold. Shadows squatted in the corners where they had no business squatting, but like silent drunks, were too harmless to justify ousting. Pins and needles made hornet-filled trees of my legs. The radiator gave its little metallic *tick-tick-tack*, and belched liquidly. Even the light, splintered by the Venetian blinds to form horizontal bars of cold fire on the puke-green wall, looked the same.

But today something *was* different. When I moved my hand down over my face, over features that had aged badly without my consent and without my noticing, the very ordinary caul of post-slumber confusion clung to the tips of my fingers, and didn't let go as I brought them up for inspection.

Like the memory of old kisses, there was a cobweb stretched across my mouth, violin-string skeins of it stretching out to my fingertips as if waiting for my horrified cry to play them. But I didn't utter a sound, even when I probed the expanse of the web with my tongue and it came away coated in sour-tasting dust.

I sat up, not without effort, and beat and pulled and scratched somewhat hysterically at my mouth until all that remained of the cobweb hung in dark brownish clumps from my fingers. *Steady, Al.* My heart was beating fast enough to give me pause, to distract me from the origin of my panic. *Calm down, it's okay, it's all right*, I told myself and waited for the voltage of fear to ebb away. *It's okay.* I looked up at the ceiling. There were cracks in the plaster and cobwebs in the corners, but none on the unremarkable light shade. Of course, there wouldn't be, for it was the obvious suspect, the inanimate villain of the piece, who had shed its cotton candy cobweb skin onto my face as I'd slept.

Grimacing, I got up, every joint and muscle firing off a round of pain, and after a careful inspection of the terrycloth for more invasive gossamer threads, crept into the robe. The smell of disinfectant, nauseatingly familiar, reached me before I opened the door, before I'd cinched the belt on my robe. The smell is meant to hide the odors of age, sickness and death, of hopelessness, but for those of us who call this place a home, it is a constant reminder that we are the creatures from which the terrible stench originates, things better hidden away so the world can be spared the inconvenience of looking at us and seeing its future.

When I got to the lounge after the usual ritual of ignoring the staff's automated cheer, and waiting for mail that wasn't there, I found my friend The Cowboy's chair was empty, and he hadn't made his move. The chess pieces were as we'd left them the evening before. The only other soul in the room was Doris Randle, who had at least been capable of a smile when she'd first been admitted, but now gaped dumbly at me as a string of drool tried to connect the corner of her mouth to her paisley-patterned bosom. Two strokes had made an empty vessel of her. It was my contention another would kill her.

"Morning Doris," I said, one hand absently moving to my mouth to be sure no trace of the cobweb remained, or maybe I feared her drooling was contagious.

She stared without seeing me.

"You know him?" she muttered, and I, mistakenly assuming

she was talking about The Cowboy, almost celebrated her words as the most coherent anyone had heard from her in months. But then "The kid?" she continued, and I let out a long low sigh. "The one in the classroom? They let the little bastard loose with his crayons. They asked him to color the heart." Her eyes grew more distant, dropped away from me to the chess set. "He didn't stay inside the lines."

I followed her gaze. Looked at the chair. It shouldn't have been empty. It never was at this time of day. Meeting here for our morning chess and banter was about the only ritual either of us had, and one we had come to depend on to help preserve our wits in a place designed, it seemed, to steal them. Then, as I stared at the cheap plastic-backed chair, envisioning The Cowboy with his small blue eyes, salt-and-pepper hair, and grizzled chin, the light through the room's single window changed, only slightly, but enough to make me think it should have been snowing outside. It was that kind of light. Cold and blue. It diffused the gnarled and sad shadow of the eucalyptus in the planter on the sill, blurring it, making the outthrust limbs look like the desperate arms of one of my fellow inmates, clambering for the sleeve of someone who might care.

I wanted to ask Doris if she had noticed the peculiar change in the room, but knew she wouldn't answer, at least not coherently. So, "You take care now," I told her, and left before she was able to coax her gaze back to where I'd been standing. A man could get lost if he spent too long wading through the overgrowth in her field of vision.

Back in the hall I grabbed the first nurse unfortunate enough to cross my path, and asked her where The Cowboy was. But even before that loathsome look of practiced sympathy crossed Nurse Stanford's taut face, I knew.

"He went peacefully," she said. "In his sleep. You must have been close."

It struck me as odd that she didn't know that. There wasn't enough camaraderie among the withered souls in Spring Grace for our friendship to have gone unnoticed. I thought of the slight chill I'd felt in the lounge, the changing of the light. Now it seemed like an omen. I almost smiled. The Cowboy would have been smugly satisfied to know that his passing had knocked askew some portion of the universe, however briefly.

"Is everything all right, Mr. Ross?"

"Yes, why?"

"No particular reason."

Then why ask? I thought, but said instead, "I'm fine. Thank you." I started to move away, then stopped and looked back. Nurse Stanford hadn't moved. She was still standing there, hands clasped matron-like beneath her bosom.

"Can you please," I said, "if it isn't too much trouble, send someone in to remove the cobwebs from my room?"

She looked momentarily confused by the request. I didn't wait for her answer. Instead I headed back to my room, and was relieved to find the light hadn't changed in my sanctuary.

I sat on the edge of the bed for a while, hands folded in my lap, feeling unpleasantly hollow deep in my chest and alarmingly near tears. Worse, I couldn't tell how much of my burgeoning sorrow was for The Cowboy, and how much was a result of the selfish realization that I was now well and truly alone.

My last remaining friend was gone.

I wondered if he had really gone quietly into the sunset, or if, before they stowed him in the back of that quiet ambulance, they'd had to pause to remove the cobwebs from his lips.

2

Noon brought thoughts of a towheaded kid who'd loved magic. A kid who used to usher his Mom and me into the living room, knowing it would mean he'd get to stay up a little later than usual. He wore a top hat and a cape. He even had the white gloves and the dramatic flourish the costume seemed to instill in whoever wore it. Those gloves cut the air above a red velvet tablecloth he'd spread across a narrow workbench. Props were arranged atop that crimson surface, sleeves shirked back, face impassive but not entirely hiding the look, the barely contained smirk that told us all we were going to be astounded and amazed, whether we believed in him or not.

Beneath the cobwebs Marcia was forever vowing to remove, little Joey called upon his carefully practiced powers of prestidigitation to stun us all, and while many of his tricks were transparent numbers, more often than not, he succeeded.

But the years robbed him of magic and the need to impress. They robbed us all of a lot of things.

He still calls from time to time, but only to assuage his guilt, and to remind himself I'm still there.

Sometimes, I don't wait for his concern to lead him.

After lunch I found myself in the hallway, lamenting my choice of the mushy Salisbury steak and wishing I had some gum, or a mint, anything to rid my palate of the noxious taste. I stepped up to the payphone after patiently listening to Zach Greenburg cursing at his daughter for fifteen minutes.

The earpiece was unpleasantly moist as I listened to the connection worming its way from Ohio to Colorado.

On the third ring, Joey answered.

"Dad? Jesus, how've you been?"

"Not good enough for you to start calling me Jesus."

His laugh was strained, as always. "Nice to hear that place hasn't knocked the wit out of you."

"Not for the want of trying."

"Right."

The stretches of silence grow longer every time we talk, as we both search for something agreeable to say. It has become like trying to find change in a phone booth's coin return. Sometimes you get lucky; more often you don't.

"So how's the weather there?" he asked.

"Sunny." *Aside from a brief change to tell me my friend had died.*

"Nice. It's cold as hell down here."

"I'd still rather be there than here. The idea of stocking up wood excites the hell out of me. Better than sitting in my room waiting for something interesting to happen."

"Yeah." Pause. The rustle of papers in the background. *Multitasking*. "It was Drew's birthday last weekend. Wish you could have been here."

"I didn't know." And in truth, resented the implication in his voice that I should have. "What is he now, nine?"

"Eleven."

I whistled.

"I've been meaning to get up there to see you, you know?"

I didn't know, but as easy—and in truth, pleasurable—as it would have been to say so, I resisted and mumbled affirmation into the phone.

"But it's a long haul, Dad. Especially with Kathy working such long hours. If she takes time off now it'll look bad. She's still in training, did I tell you that?"

"No." Nor did I know what she was in training *for*.

"Yeah. If she took time off, it'd set her back, and she's busted her hump long enough."

"Why not come up here by yourself? Get me out of this dump for a night and tie one on with your old man? Like we did back in—"

"Dad?"

"What?"

"Dad? Yeah. Can you hold on, just a sec? I got a call coming in that I need to take. Seriously. Stay with me OK? I promise... just a sec."

"All r—"

An abrupt click and the phone became a conch shell, whispering to me in the voice of my own blood.

I waited ten minutes, maybe a little less, certainly no more, before I hung up.

He didn't call back, and I knew better than to wait.

3

That Friday, our prison was invaded by a group of high school students, led by a petite raven-haired and bespectacled teacher who seemed convinced she could alter the world and, more specifically, the universes of her charges, with frantic gesticulation and a series of high-pitched yelps. They orbited around her like lazily drifting planets until she meted out their destinations and observed them as they spun off into the hall. While she directed the flow of angst-ridden traffic, we stared with the same kind of fascination a tired dog uses to watch birds eating the crumbs from his bowl.

"Joseph Henner," the teacher wailed. "I know that's not a lighter I just saw in your hand. Make your way to Mr. Ross's room. Number 18; end of the hall. Remember why we're here."

Why we're here. I was still waiting for someone to let *me* in on that little secret. I hurried back to my room.

Henner skulked in a few moments later. He was a scrawny acne-riddled teen dressed in a black trenchcoat, scuffed Doc Martens and a T-shirt that displayed a skull-headed man wielding a knife beneath the legend: *We All Gotta Go Sometime. Some of Us Sooner Than Others.*

True enough, I thought.

"What school do you go to?" I asked him, when it became painfully clear he wasn't going to initiate the conversation.

"Crosby High."

A quip about the absence of Stills and Nash from the name rose in my mind like an image in a photographer's developer tray, but I let it pass. Any hope was ludicrous that the sullen mass of baggy clothes and attitude before me would have even the slightest idea what I was referring to.

"I'm Joe," he said.

"Alfred Ross."

"Cool." He didn't look at me. "So, do you, like, stay here all the time?"

"Yes."

"That blows. Doesn't it get boring?"

"Absolutely."

"I'd go nuts."

"Some of us have."

"You got a TV?"

"Sure, in the lounge. And my friend and I play chess." I caught myself too late and felt my polite smile fade. "Used to play chess."

"He die?"

"Yes. Just last night as a matter of fact."

"How?"

Only then, only in that very instant, with the rest home filled with the alien sound of youthful laughter and this morose kid inspecting my room and talking about death like it was an old television show he only vaguely remembered, did I realize I didn't know how The Cowboy had died. *In his sleep*, Nurse Stanford had said, and it had been enough at the time. It wasn't enough now.

Cobwebs got his heart.

"Old age," I said, at last, and knew it wasn't a lie.

"Bummer."

"Yeah. It is. He was a good friend."

"So..." he began as he looked around my room, at the bare picture-less walls and the half-full glass of water sitting on my nightstand, "How long you been here?" It sounded like something he was reading from a cue card, and all the while he avoided looking at me. Maybe he was afraid he'd see a vision of himself in sixty years.

I could have assured him that I'm nobody's future.

"Coming up on six years."

"Long time."

"Feels longer," I said, and that was the God's honest truth. It felt like the tail end of a life sentence.

The kid sighed. His patience wasn't going to hold out much longer, and I couldn't really blame him. At his age humoring old folks would have been way down at the bottom of my priority list too.

At length his gaze settled on the only picture in my room, the grainy, washed-out photograph of Meredith on the windowsill.

"Your wife?"

"Ex."

"Still alive?"

"Yes, and cavorting with the pool boys in Florida, I imagine."

He asked an odd question then, one that, given his demeanor, I'd never have expected to hear from him: "You still love her?" It was also the only question he asked during our short time together that sounded as if the answer mattered to him.

Why, I'd never know.

"Yes. She's my biggest regret. Letting her go, that is."

"Then why did you?"

"I didn't have much of a say in the matter."

He nodded, ran a finger over the cheap faux-gold frame, and I knew I'd lost whatever spark of interest had flared in him. "You have any war stories?"

"No, I never fought in any wars. Do you?"

"Do I what?"

"Have any war stories."

He jammed his hands into his pockets. "Dude...I'm in high school."

"Isn't that a type of battlefield?"

Shrug. "Whatever."

Outcast, I thought. *Probably slouches in the corners at school trying to avoid trouble, rock music blasting in his ears, then goes home and does the same there, avoids life as much as possible. Hides in his shell.*

I felt sorry for him until I realized my life wasn't a whole lot different. Both of us were in cages of different design, but cages all the same.

"How come you've only got one picture?"

"I have more. I keep them under the bed. Would you like to see them?" Only after the words were out of my mouth did I realize how creepy they sounded. I might as well have propositioned the poor kid. *Hey boy, want some candy?* Inwardly, I groaned.

"Nah. Some other time."

"We don't have to talk, y'know," I told him. "You can just tell your teacher we did."

"Suits me," he said without hesitation, and produced from his trench coat pocket a pair of earphones so small I wondered if he'd ever had to reel them out of his inner ear. A small white rectangle with silver buttons followed and he jabbed at it with a nicotine-stained forefinger. The earphones began to hiss.

It felt wrong not to say something else, for the boy looked lost, crumpled up inside himself, desperate perhaps, the true emotion in his eyes obscured by the steam from the anger at the core of him. Maybe I should have been firm instead of grandfatherly. Maybe I should have told him to sit up straight and tell me what his problem was, to have some respect for his elders. Maybe that's what he was missing in his life, someone who looked like they gave enough of a damn to listen to what he had to say. But by the time enlightenment chased away the fog in my brain, Henner had already plugged his ears and thumbed up the volume on his odd-looking player.

"Later, man," he said as he stood up and headed for the door, the angry wasp sound of the music trailing behind him.

"What will happen then?" I murmured as he stepped out into the hall, into the river of students and moved upstream against the current.

I wondered how long it would take for him to erase me and my sad little room with its single picture from his mind.

• • •

There was a headcount in the hall sometime later, a chorus of bored responses, and then the roar of a bus engine signaled the departure of youthful laughter from Spring Grace. I trudged to the lounge, took my usual seat at the small Formica table The Cowboy and I always shared. The chess set was still there, but someone had prematurely ended our game and set up the pieces for a new one.

"Ron," I called to a tall thin man in a chenille robe, who was sitting in a worn armchair and grumbling at the television. "Ron!" His shock of white hair rose above the back of the armchair like stuffing.

He looked over his shoulder, his silver stubble scratching against the robe, and gaped fish-like at me through bifocal lenses. "*What* for God's sake?"

"You play chess?"

"What?"

I resisted the urge to scream at him. "Chess. Do you play it?"

"Like checkers, isn't it?"

"No. Not really."

"Then, no," he said, and turned back to his show. "I don't."

No one else present in the lounge did either, and by the time I'd put the question to them all, I didn't feel much like playing anymore. Besides, when The Cowboy and I had played, it hadn't really been about the game.

"He could never do clouds." Doris was sitting by the window, staring out, her eyes like pale gems in the deep pockets of a thief. "They were always dark and crooked, even when the sky was right. Liked to draw the spiders. Made them look like small men crouching in the corners."

"Sounds like a real talented boy," I told her, but knew I was talking to myself. Still, it made me curious, as it always did, to know who it was that had ownership of such a prized lot in her brain that not even her strokes could turn it fallow, or salt the earth of recollection. Whoever it was, whether real or fantasy, living or dead, they would not truly die until she did. And for that, I envied them.

● ● ●

Summer tired of its sun and dance routine, and moved on. The leaves died and the voice of the wind grew hollow, playing discordant music through the eaves of Spring Grace. The sense of isolation deepened. People stayed in their houses, and we in our rooms. A few more of my neighbors passed away. Some in their sleep; some screaming, while people whispered in the hall. Others were ferried away in the night in the quiet ambulances and never seen again. I told myself they'd escaped, been granted a stay of execution and were enjoying their freedom somewhere warm, but inside I knew better. Nobody ever leaves this place, though we talk about it all the time. *The door's right there*, we'd say, *and no one would even notice if we walked straight outta here.* And yet we never do. In times of excitement, that door looks like the door to Heaven. More often, it looks like the opposite.

We don't know what's out there anymore, you see. At some point none of us can remember, we stepped off the train and it carried on without us. Years have passed, been stolen while we've slept, and beyond our windows the world has changed. The light has changed.

It's safer here, even if it means we have to endure the ghosts of our pasts, the specters of regret, with nary a distraction to keep us sane. It's safer here because the future is guaranteed. There are no surprises left for us within these walls. You pass the time. You smile at kindred spirits in the hall. Maybe one weekend you luck out and end up getting your hands on the remote control before anyone else, maybe get to watch a Western or an old MGM musical. And at night, in bed, you say a small urgent prayer to a God you don't believe in that you'll wake in the morning still in possession of all those things that have made you what you are. That you won't find yourself dazed and drooling in a chair next to Doris Randle, with the needle in your mind stuck in a groove. But most of all, you pray that someone out there still remembers you, still thinks about you every now and then...still loves you, because there isn't a dark memory or shard of guilt inside that terrifies you as much as the idea of being forgotten. *Please*, you whisper, knowing tonight might be the night that quiet ambulance comes for you, its brakes squeaking softly as it pulls up to the curb. *Please...remember me.*

And as sleep comes, you remember *them*, and all the things you did wrong that led you to this place, this desert island forever threatened by the encroaching tide of time and regret. You weep, and in the morning the cobwebs on your face are larger, denser than before.

"We did clean your room, Mr. Ross. I sent one of the orderlies in there yesterday while you were having dinner."

"Then they did a sloppy job."

"Are you feeling all right? You look pale. Maybe I should—"

"I'm fine. I need to use the phone. Please have someone go over my room again."

"Of course."

• • •

He didn't mention the last call. I doubted he even remembered it.

"Dad? Great news. I sold a screenplay to Bob Garrison at New Line."

"New Line? What's that, like the fishing channel?"

A chuckle. "It's a Hollywood film company. We're talking *big* time here."

"I see, well congratulations then."

"You don't sound impressed."

My fingers tightened on the phone. I looked over my shoulder and saw Zach Greenburg scowling at me, oxygen mask gripped tightly in one liver-spotted hand. His rheumy eyes radiated impatience. He was no doubt anxious to call his daughter for her bi-weekly lecture. I turned back to the phone.

"It's not that, it's...why haven't you been in touch?"

"I tried a few times. No one answered."

It was a lie, a poor one, and it hollowed me out like a Jack o' Lantern. The phone doesn't ring enough in Spring Grace for it to ever go unanswered. But I accepted it because the alternatives were no better. What did I want to hear? *Dad, I forgot. Sorry.* No, I would take the lie. A starving man can't afford to be choosy about the quality of meat he's given. Unless it's Salisbury steak.

"Okay," I said. "Any plans to come see me?"

"Sure, we'll work something out."

"It's been forever."

"It has. Dad, I'll get up there, I promise. This new deal will mean I'll have to travel to New York now and then. I can stop in to see you on the way back."

"That would be nice. You should bring Kathy and Drew along too."

A sigh. "Maybe. We'll see."

"Is everything all right with you guys?"

"It's fine. You'll see us soon, I promise."

Behind me, Zach shuffled his feet.

"Listen Joey, I have to get going. There's a queue for the phone forming here."

"Okay Dad. Thanks for calling. It's always good to hear from you."

"You too. Stay in touch, will you? Call anytime. It's not like I'm busy around here."

"Will do."

"Give my love to my grandson."

"Bye Dad."

I hung up and as fast as his stiff joints would allow, Zach was in my face, his breath like sour milk, hooked nose inches from mine. "How do you do that?"

I raised my hands, not to placate him, but to remind him there was such a thing as personal space and that he was invading mine. "Do what?"

"Make calls without using money? There a trick to it?"

I looked over my shoulder at the phone, as if the answer to his odd question might be written somewhere there. It was a basic model payphone, silver, with square touchtone buttons. "Collect," I told him after a moment of thought. "Dial zero first, then the number."

He considered this, then nodded sharply. "Wish someone had told me that when I first got here. I've been stealin' nickels for six years." His laugh turned into a coughing fit, then a series of strangled gasps. I waited a moment to be sure he wasn't going to end up dropping dead right there, then left him, red-faced and wheezing, but well enough to complain about the contaminants "those goddamned witches" were putting in his oxygen. After poking my head into my room to ensure the nurse had made good on her vow to have the cobwebs removed (she had), I stared down at my slippers as they traced the same old route back to the lounge.

There could be grass under there, I thought, with a faint smile, *gravel or macadam. I'm the only thing keeping me here. There are plenty of people out there who I can get to know. People who would think of me as a friend, maybe, or a kindly neighbor. People who'd remember me.* And as I passed the glass doors of the main entrance and ignored the pleasant inquiry from the pretty young nurse at the station, my smile grew.

Elm trees lined the long straight path from the door to the street, which in turn led into town. A couple of dozen steps and I could hitch a ride. A couple of steps; a short walk. That was all. Anyone could make it. *I* could make it. Abruptly I was assailed by memories from my youth: of walking barefoot through the grass with my best friend Rusty O' Connor, as oblivious to the mosquitoes as I was to the nurse who spoke to me as if I'd magically reverted to the age represented in the memory. Fishing poles held by our sides, the backs of our necks reddened by the glaring sun, laughing our fool heads off at silly things as we headed for Myers Pond and the promise of catfish we would never catch. The rumble and scrape of trains beyond the pond; the honk of jaybirds warning its brethren of our approach; the low buzz of dragonflies beating us to the shimmering water...

"Mr. Ross?"

A cloud darkened the sun of memory; the color faded, as did the smile it had brought to my face. Out there lay the road, but where did the road lead? To a new life or an overdue death? Rusty had followed a path in his dotage that had erased him from the earth, never to be seen again, nothing but a cryptic message left behind to let his wife know he wouldn't be coming back. Did he choose the wrong road? Did he stand on a similar threshold, lured by the promise of something better? Of a few more years of adventure?

"Mr. Ross? Is everything all right?"

Did he go somewhere he thought he'd be remembered?

"I'm fine," I said curtly, sensing the nurse moving around the desk toward me.

Outside, beyond the glass that might as well have been an iron gate, the elm trees nodded slightly in the breeze. They almost seemed to whisper, *Foolish old man. Remember your place.*

I moved on, watching my feet tread nothing but worn tile, just like yesterday, and a thousand days before it.

Do a trick for me, Joey, I thought, with tears in my throat. *Make me vanish. I'd rather be where you are.*

• • •

The man seated at the chess set looked out of place in the lounge. He was dressed like a salesman, from his paisley blazer and yellow shirt, right down to his white socks and worn leather loafers. Beneath a thick head of curly black hair, equally thick eyebrows were knitted in concentration over a pair of silver-rimmed spectacles. His long, oddly delicate and perfectly manicured fingers floated above the head of the unsuspecting black queen.

I sat down with an audible sigh, glad to be relieved of my own weight for a while. "Doctor."

He looked up and beamed. "Mr. Ross. How are we this morning?"

"Tired."

As per usual, Ron had commandeered the television and seemed hypnotized by the gymnastic bounce of a female prize-winner's breasts on some game show. I couldn't blame him really. They were far from proportionate, given the woman's slight build.

"Are you still taking your medication?"

I nodded, turning my attention to Doris. She sat in her preferred spot by the window, head tilted as if asleep, but her eyes were still open. She looked more distant than ever. While Ron gaped at his buxom contestant, I found myself watching Doris's chest to be sure she was still breathing.

"She's okay," Doctor Rhodes said.

"Good." I turned to face the board. "Do you play?"

"Not since high school I'm afraid."

"Good enough. It'll still put you leagues above anyone else in here."

He looked at me over the rims of his spectacles. "Except you."

"Except me."

"Wonderful."

I studied the white ranks before me. "The AMA relaxing their dress code?" I nodded pointedly at his atrocious suit.

He smiled and folded his arms. "It's my day off."

"And you're spending it here?"

He shrugged and blew out a breath. "Well, I've been so busy with administrative work lately, I thought it the perfect opportunity to come in and see how people were doing."

I smirked at him and advanced a pawn. "That's very sad, Doc."

"Not at all," he protested. "When was the last chance you and I had a chance to shoot the breeze?"

He copied my move, but I didn't watch it. I was too busy watching him, trying to read his face, but his pleasant expression was an effective shield.

"I hate to disappoint you," I said, moving my bishop into the space the pawn had vacated. "But I very much doubt anything of any consequence has occurred since we last spoke."

Again he copied my move. "Is that so?" He was moving toward a point and his refusal to make it was starting to annoy me, but not nearly as much as the sensation that unseen hands were slowly painting a target on my head.

"I get the feeling you don't agree."

He smiled warmly and flapped a hand at me. "Ah, it's nothing."

"Then why are you here?"

"Well..." He looked around the room, his gaze lingering on Doris longer than it had on any of the other occupants, until finally his eyes met mine. "I can't let even the most innocuous of incidences go unquestioned around here, Alfred, you can understand that. The risk is too high to just pass it off as the vagaries of old age."

My fingers had settled on the bishop. Now they released it, unmoved.

Rhodes seemed to be searching for the right words to say what he'd come to say, and I willed him to spit them out. At length, he did.

"Nurse Stanford mentioned some weeks ago that you were shaken up by what happened to Harold Wayne—The Cowboy—is that right?"

"I was." I frowned at him, saw uncertainty flicker across his face. My unease increased. "Why? Does that make me cause for concern? A special case? He was my friend. One of the few I have...I *had* in here. Naturally losing him would shake me up, just as it would anyone else." I became aware that my voice had risen above conversational level and I was being needlessly defensive. Ron's chair creaked as he finally looked away from the game show and peered at us. Some of the men at a card table in the corner paused to watch. I dismissed them all with a disgusted wave of my hand and glared at Rhodes. "Why? And why are you looking at me like that?"

He clasped his hands together over the chessboard. "I'm worried about you, and I don't think you're telling me the truth about you taking your pills."

"Of course I am. I said I was, didn't I? And what are you worried about me for anyway?"

"I'm worried, Alfred, because The Cowboy died over four years ago."

I stared at him. He stared back, the concern in his eyes maddening. Insulting.

"You *know* that," he said in a low voice as he reached across the table, his sleeve scattering the pieces as he tried to take my hand. I pulled away from him.

"Why would you say that?"

"Because it's the truth. A truth you know, and have known for years. He died in his sleep on Christmas Eve. You were the one who found him, remember? It was snowing like crazy outside. Worst snowstorm we'd had in decades."

Cold blue light, a voice tried to insist but I slammed the door shut on it, just as I intended to slam the door shut on Rhodes and his lies. "Why are you...?" I shook my head. "I won't tolerate this. Not from you, or anyone else. You have no right."

"Alfred, listen..."

"No." I rose and winced as a bolt of pain slammed into my right knee. I braced a hand on the chair to steady myself. "I don't know what it is you're trying to accomplish with this madness, but I won't sit here and listen to it. It's one of the few privileges I have left."

I began to hobble toward the door, heard the sound of chair legs scraping against the floor as Rhodes stood.

Go, Alfred, I told myself, my arms and legs trembling so bad I was afraid I wouldn't make it to the door, *Go before he tells you the rest. Go before he tells you what happened to—*

I froze.

The room itself seemed to send waves of cold air at me, chilling my back through my shirt while heat blossomed in my chest, stealing my breath. Tears welled in my eyes. Unseen fingers squeezed my throat.

I will not hear this. I will not.

The sound of rubber soles slapping against tile and all of a sudden Nurse Stanford was standing in the doorway, blocking my way.

Despite the pain that drilled through me from the top of my skull down into my chest, I almost laughed, though on some distant level I doubted I had the strength. *It's an intervention.*

"You've been using the phone," Rhodes said, and his voice was close, cautious. "Can I ask who you've been calling?"

"My..." My breath burned in my throat. "...Son."

"Alfred...the box beneath your bed..."

"Don't touch it."

"No one has."

"Then...how do you know?"

The cheers from the television were muted. The compassion on Nurse Stanford's face made me want to throttle her, but even if I had the guts to attempt such a thing, my arms refused to move. I felt a tear trickle down my cheek.

"How do I know *what*, Alfred?" He moved to stand in front of me, but his shadow was a second too slow in following.

The fluorescent lights covered my eyes with frost as I felt the strength drain from my limbs. *I'm going to fall and they won't catch me*, I thought, pure terror surging up through me from a bottomless pit in my stomach. *I'll hit my head and die right here in this awful room with all these people here staring at—*

My mind buzzed, chased away the pain, the thought, the awareness. I turned, intending to run, driven by one last automatic impulse to flee from these insane people—

—and fell forward, tried to think my arms into action, but they stayed by my sides. I toppled like the pawns beneath the Doctor's sleeve.

● ● ●

A heart attack, the man in the quiet ambulance told me. *But you'll be fine*, he said.

I know different.

I've lost them all. Their faces only exist now beneath my bed, in the box that has been substituting for memory. Black and white photographs, snapshots, obituaries, and letters from long-silenced voices I have been hearing on the phone.

Doctor Rhodes stopped by in the beginning, to check on me, but as time went by his commitment to the residents at Spring Grace caused his visits to become infrequent. I haven't seen him in almost a month. I have a new doctor now. New nurses, whose faces aren't so sharp or smiles as false. I have a new room.

It has no window.

This frightens me. Because there will come a night when the

small men crouching in the corners come out, dancing like lunatics, and maybe one of those small men will be wearing white gloves, and his hands will cut the air above a red velvet tablecloth, and he'll do one last magic trick for me. He'll make endless veils of cobwebs fall from the ceiling and they'll land like muslin on my face. Over and over and over again until my breath stops coming and my heart stops beating. He'll hide me as I have hidden him for so long.

But not yet. I am not done yet.

Not tonight.

There is a sullen high school boy out there who still might remember. There is a sour old man with an oxygen mask back at Spring Grace, who is thankful he no longer has to wait in line. There is a drooling woman who speaks in riddles, who has a golden field in her mind where the people she has known still run.

Maybe I'm there.

Maybe she remembers.

Maybe.

LETTING GO

BY M P JOHNSON

Janie wished she could get into an argument with her son. She wished he would shout, "I'm never talking to you again," and disappear from her life for a year like other peoples' kids did, usually after some minor parental transgression, like a judgmental comment about a love interest or career choice or tattoo. But her son, 26 years old with the mind of a two-year-old, would never get tattoos, start a career or find love, other than that which Janie provided, so she didn't even have an opportunity to get into an argument. Tad would never disappear.

She stood over the stove, sweating and feeling guilty for thinking such a thing, even as Tad screamed from the kitchen table, fists gloppy with mashed potatoes. No matter how many times her frustration drove her to the same thought, she always felt guilty about it.

"I should bring you back to the home, Taddy." She said the words knowing he didn't understand, just to feel the guilt turn them to briars in her throat. She had handed him over to Care Forever three times over the years. Each time, not even a month passed before she rescued him. Tad's cries had haunted her dreams while he was away. She had nightmares of his wiry, 140-pound body strapped down and jabbed with hot pokers by orderlies. She couldn't keep him, but she couldn't entrust him to anyone else, so where did that leave her? Wishing, that's where.

Wishing things were different.

"They're trained professionals, Janie," her brother Jeremy had said. He had talked her into sending Tad away each time. "You're a single mother. It's best for both of you."

"Fuck you, brother," she said under her breath now as she slid her hamburger out of the pan and onto a plate. Jeremy didn't know what was best for her or Tad. How could he? Like everyone else in her life – like Tad's pathetic father, like all her worthless friends – he had retreated, as if Tad's condition was contagious. He lived less than five miles away, but only stopped by once a year. He and his beautiful family couldn't even be bothered to invite Janie and Tad over for Christmas. "It's just too stressful," he once told her.

As she sat down and took a bite out of the second burger she had made for herself that evening, she couldn't disagree. Tad had thrown her first burger, and his, out the window. For a moment, she had marveled at his aim. She had long ago stopped hoping in moments like those that he would suddenly get better and become a pro baseball player. If a miracle were going to happen, it would have happened already.

"Booger!" Tad bellowed, reaching for Janie's plate.

"I made you a burger already, Taddy. Remember what happened to it?"

He sucked the mashed potatoes off his thin fingers, staring out the window.

"You threw it out the window, didn't you?"

"Throw!" His gray eyes brightened.

Sometimes, when she was angry with him, she thought about how he looked 10 years younger than he had any right to, while she looked that much older than her 47 years, and she would silently curse him for stealing her youth. Then her stomach would acid up with guilt and she would push the thought away.

Occasionally, she would run into strangers at the grocery store or gas station who would comment, "You're so patient with him," and she wanted to slap them. What choice did she have? She had spent years trying to yell at him, trying to spank him into doing what he couldn't possibly do, into understanding what his brain would never allow him to understand. That had gotten her nowhere.

"Booger," he screamed again, as if that was the only thing in this world he had ever wanted. Somewhere under his scream, she heard something in the basement. How good she had gotten at normalizing a noise that would make others' ears ring. Hushing him, she listened. She heard a definite skittering downstairs.

"Rats," she said.

"Boooooooooger!" Tad replied, so intensely the vein in his forehead pulsed.

Janie laughed. "If I give you this burger, will you eat it nice?"

Tad's entire body shook.

She slid the plate across the table. He sank his teeth in, chewing slowly.

"Is that good?"

"Ummmmm," he answered, as his fingers danced the burger out of its bun and he took another bite of the well-done ground beef patty.

Then he hurled it out the window.

The lump of feces in the corner of the basement, where cinderblock walls met poured concrete floors, didn't look right to Janie. Too green. Too rigid. When she poked it with a wire coat hanger, it reminded her of dissecting owl pellets in school. Bones hid inside, the bones of other rats. Half-digested eyeballs stared at her shyly, black and shiny, as if self-conscious about being found in such a place.

"Great." She sighed. "Not only do I have rats, I have cannibal rats."

She cleaned up the mess immediately. Despite the holes in the walls, the duct-taped lamps and stained carpet, she prided herself on keeping the little bungalow as clean as possible for her and Tad.

She put down rat traps. Each held a block of cheese that she hated to part with. She worked part time at the care center, having lucked out finding a job that doubled as daycare. Tad got disability money from the government too. Even so, she found herself pressed for cash more often than not and struggling to keep the fridge stocked. As skinny as he was, Tad's metabolism ran high. Sometimes she wished he was like the fat, docile kids at the care center. Her life might have been easier. Then she thought about their fat, docile mothers and decided she preferred her own body, the muscles she had built. On one of her many first dates, the man noticed her forearms and challenged her to an arm-wrestling match, which she won. He had been excited by her strength, until she explained that, no, she hadn't spent any time in the gym lifting weights. She had earned the muscle the hard way, restraining her son during his fits. She never saw that man again.

"Momma!" Tad cried from upstairs.

Hearing a crash, she took the steps two at a time, knowing that a second could make the difference between having to buy a new piece of furniture or not. In the living room, she found Tad smashing the family portrait – the two of them posed and smiling in the best clothes they could afford. He had put another hole in the wall and the dust clouded the room. Not his usual outburst, which typically involved throwing the TV remote or couch cushions, but certainly not unprecedented.

"Momma!" he screamed.

She grabbed the shattered picture frame out of his hands, threw it aside and wrapped her arms around him from behind. His shaking became her shaking. She held tight. This was not one of her son's typical angry outbursts at all. This was not driven by that gaudy red puppet Oomo not coming on TV or him not getting a second helping of dessert. Something had scared him.

"What is it, Taddy?" she asked, still holding him as he kicked wildly, adding to the collection of bruises on her shins.

"Amal, Momma! Amal!"

"An animal? You saw an animal?"

Was it a rat? Would that scare Tad so much? He shrieked and she fell to the ground exhausted, still clenching him in her arms, pulling him into her lap. Tears streaked down his cheeks. He shook so hard and she held him as tight as she could.

She realized she was crying too.

"I need you to come over, Jeremy. I've got rats," Janie said, sitting in a lawn chair in her sunny little backyard as Tad chased around after a big blue ball with Oomo's smiling face on it.

"Did you set traps?"

"Yep, two days ago, but they haven't done any good. I was hoping you could come over and find where they're holed up. You know I'm no good at that stuff," she lied. She would have been able to do it herself, just like she had installed the new light fixture in the bathroom after Tad pulled the old one out of the wall. Just like she had done everything she needed to do since Tad was born.

"Kelly and I have to run to the mall."

"Do you remember when we would go to the woods out by the airport after school? You always managed to find a skink hive and pull out a lizard, or at least its tail. You and I were inseparable then. I looked up to you because you were so brave. I thought for sure you could find this rat. By the size of its shi… poop, it's pretty big."

"This trip to the mall just can't wait."

She hung up the phone, wishing that after all this time the hurt would have dulled. But it hadn't. Every time she asked Jeremy to be there for her and he gave her an excuse it felt exactly the same. She wished she hadn't even asked, but she always did, and she always would. Even though she knew he was an asshole.

"Momma!" Tad yelled. "Catch!"

He threw the ball. It arced high but soared directly into her hands as if pulled to them. Her son could barely get a forkful of food into his mouth without getting it on his cheeks. She didn't understand how he could throw with such accuracy.

"Good throw, Taddy!"

"Good throw!" he repeated, clapping his hands.

He flashed his million-dollar smile, as she liked to call it, pulling his chin tight into his neck and grinning so wide it seemed to spread out through his whole body, into the air around him. She gave him a kiss on his forehead, running her hand over his buzz cut.

"Good throw, Taddy!" he shouted again.

As Tad bounced on the couch and sang along to songs blaring from the TV, songs he had sang along to for most of his life, songs that had long since become scars on Janie's brain, she snuck down to the basement.

She had replaced the moldy cheese with peanut butter, but still the traps remained unsprung. As if to taunt her, her guests had left another present, in the same corner as before. Little bones stuck out of it.

This time though, her guests hadn't been as clean. They had stepped in their waste, leaving a trail of shitty footprints. She inspected them carefully. They seemed so big, each as long as her pointer finger. Sharp toes jutted outward instead of forward, as if bowlegged. Was that what rat footprints looked like?

She followed the trail, which she realized was made by a single animal, past the washer and dryer to a pile of boxes stacked on the opposite side of the basement. Clearing them aside, she expected to find some sort of nest. Instead, she found a hole in the cinderblocks – two feet wide, a foot high and rough around the edges, as if gnawed. It couldn't have been gnawed though. Rats didn't gnaw through concrete. The blocks must have crumbled with age.

She ran the tip of her finger around the rat hole. It came away soaked in gelatinous amber muck. Dripping from her fingertip, the goop smelled like urine. She wiped it on the floor and ran upstairs to make an appointment with an exterminator.

Janie woke in the middle of the night to the sound of Tad screaming. Her eyes opened and without hesitation she ran from her bedroom to his. It wasn't maternal instinct that told her something was wrong; it was logic. Tad hadn't had fits at night since she started giving him sleeping pills before bed so many years ago. He always slept soundly.

When she stepped into his room, she thought she was having a nightmare. It wouldn't have been the first time she had dreamed of Tad getting maimed, usually as a result of something she did: sending him to the home, turning her back on him at a busy intersection, leaving a knife on the kitchen counter.

But this wasn't a dream. Real blood spurted out of Tad's hand where his thumb used to be, soaking into his worn plaid sheets. The rest of his fingers wiggled independently, as if trying to break free so they could hunt for their lost brother.

Janie's legs turned into balloons and burst under her, sending her to the ground. A voice in her head hissed accusingly at her: "What did you do?" Had she left a knife out? She had tried so hard for so many years, how could she have slipped up now? Had she grown that weary of taking care of her son?

She could worry about that later. Standing, she stripped off her nightgown and wrapped it around Tad's bleeding hand. He had shit the bed, and for once she couldn't blame it on his condition.

"What happened, Taddy?"

"Amal!"

"An animal?" Was that possible? Could that rat have taken Tad's thumb? It wasn't a particularly big thumb, but still. How big was the rat? She tried not to visualize the thing as she cleaned Tad's waste, dressed him and herself, and sped to the hospital to have his hand stitched up.

On the way home, groggy from painkillers and whatever remnants of the sleeping pill still swam through his blood, Tad seemed more curious about his missing digit than anything. He kept poking at the stitches, forcing Janie to take one hand off the wheel to hold his wound away from him and his scratching nails. He fell asleep before she pulled into the driveway. She carried him inside and tucked him into her bed. She wouldn't be able to sleep anyway. Changing his bloody, shitty sheets could wait.

Grabbing a broom and a kitchen knife, she tiptoed down to the basement. She would get that rat. She didn't need traps. At the bottom of the steps, she pulled the worn shoestring and the single bare light bulb flickered on.

Part of her wanted to charge the rat hole and just start stabbing. Instead, she decided to give the rodent a moment to get comfortable in case the light had startled it. Strolling around the room, she gazed at the unsprung traps, the peanut butter having attracted nothing more than dust.

In the corner, she found another pile of shit. This time though, it wasn't the cleaned bones of other rats that burst through the seams. This time, it was Tad's thumb, pointing straight up. The thumbs up gesture. It had little skin left, mostly around the nail, which must not have agreed with the rat's digestion.

Mothers often talk of maternal instinct, as if it was a normal, natural thing. There was nothing normal or natural about the sudden surge of violence Janie felt upon seeing her son's shat out digit, nor could she claim that it came from a place of love. As much "You hurt my son" fury as she would have liked to have felt, the reality was that the fury she felt was of the "You made things worse" variety. Tad wouldn't be able to wipe himself without his thumb. It would take him years to get used to it. That was years of shit wiping she would have to do, because of this fucking rat.

Now she charged. Now she ran across the room, sliding toward the rat hole, hoping to catch the rodent off guard. The move skinned her knees, but she didn't feel it. She thrust the broom handle into the cinderblock chasm. All four feet of it went in, surprising her. She poked around, trying to feel how deep it went.

She couldn't find an end.

"Jeremy, a rat ate Tad's thumb off."
"What?"
"I'm not joking. It's gone. He has nine fingers."
"I don't think that's possible."

"Well I'm not imagining it, Jeremy."

"That is awful. Poor Tad. What can I do?"

"Just come over. Just come to see Tad. And me."

"Things have been pretty crazy at the office. Tax season."

When Janie answered the door, the man on her dilapidated front steps locked eyes with her. The exterminator easily had a decade on her, but he wore his years well, much better than she wore hers. He had held onto his jet black hair, except for fingers of silver that jutted up from around his ears. She saw them as guides for where to place her hands when she pressed her lips against his, which she did, at least in her mind. He moved closer, hinted at a smile and said, "I'm your hero, angel."

At that moment, when her heart opened once again to the possibility of romance and her brain started devising ways to keep this man in her life for longer than the span of one rat execution, Tad jumped up from the living room couch and breathed through his nose so hard that two ropes of snot exploded from his nostrils, past his mouth, to hang from his chin.

"Show me where the rat is," the exterminator said, that hint of smile fading, that gleam in his eyes packing up for another day.

Janie sighed and led the man to the basement.

"You say it took the boy's thumb?"

"You believe me?"

"Fishermen, they like to tell stories. So do exterminators. The difference is, the things exterminators see, we lie to make them more believable. We exaggerate the other way. If we talked truthfully about the things we see in basements, warehouses, sewers… nobody would sleep at night."

"I'm not going to sleep at night for a while."

The exterminator scanned the cinderblocks. "This is a very clean basement."

"I try to keep it that way."

"No, I mean it's not right. This isn't what a basement this old should look like. These blocks are too new. This space is too small. Where's the hole?"

She pushed the boxes aside.

He lowered himself to his knees and pulled a little flashlight out of his pocket. Its brightness surprised Janie. It made the whole room brighter. When he pointed it into the rat hole and took a glance, he turned it off immediately and looked at her with a baffled glaze over his face. "I'm gonna need a beer."

She nodded and ran upstairs to the kitchen, stopping to use the restroom on the way. When she got back to the basement, cold one in hand, the exterminator and his bright light were gone. She should have seen it coming based on his reaction to Tad, but she had hoped the promise of a paycheck would keep him from fleeing the minute she turned her back. No such luck. Why was everyone so put off by Tad?

Of all people, she knew the answer to that question. She knew.

Tad threw a fit and she lost track of time, so she didn't get around to calling the exterminator company until the next day. The wrath she laid down on the secretary at the other end of the line would have been legendary, had she not been so tired. Instead, all she could muster was, "What kind of shoddy operation are you running over there? Your guy ran off in the middle of the job!"

"If it makes you feel any better, it seems as though Martin ran off altogether," the secretary replied, frazzled. "Now I've got to call people and tell them they'll have to wait a day or two, while they've got what they think are rabid vermin chewing up their cupboards. The best I can do for you, ma'am, is an 'I'm sorry.' Set some more traps. We'll send someone out in a day or two."

She hung up the phone. Tad stood behind her. Actually, Tad never really stood. He shifted his weight from one leg to the other, manipulating every muscle in his fingers, staring at the missing one.

"Not hurt," he said.

"It doesn't hurt anymore, Taddy?"

"No more."

She grabbed his hand and felt it loosen in hers, as if her touch was all it took to calm him. She raised the bandaged stump to her lips and kissed it.

"Amal took."

"Yes, an animal took it, a rat."

"Rat!"

"And we are going to make sure that rat doesn't come back, okay?"

"Okay!"

He followed Janie into the kitchen. She flipped through her cupboards. What could she put in the traps to draw the rodent out? Not cheese. Not peanut butter. What then? Stale cereal and dusty cans of baked beans? She cringed. She could hardly bring herself to eat most of it. Perhaps the rat was as discriminating.

"Amal took," Tad reminded her, waving his incomplete hand in her face.

She slapped it away. "I know, Taddy."

"Amal took!" he shouted, on the verge of a fit.

She kneeled down to look him in the eyes. Before she could say anything, he repeated himself and whipped open the refrigerator door. Inside, she saw the cheap ground beef that Tad had enjoyed hurling out the window.

"Good thinking! It's not human fingers, but it might do the trick," she said. "You wait here, Taddy. I'll go load the traps."

The basement smelled like meat already, meat and shit. She found another deposit in the same corner, this one containing strands of silver hair, rat hair. The rest of the rat community would thank her for ridding them of their cannibal brother. If this was, in fact, a rat. She had seen nothing but footprints, and she wasn't sure those were from a rat. Tad had simply called it an "animal." He called babies "animals." But what else could it be? A raccoon? A possum? Seemed unlikely.

It had to be a big, ugly rat.

She slapped blobs of meat onto the traps, not bothering to remove the fetid peanut butter crackers. When she had filled the traps to her satisfaction, she dropped to her hands and knees to inspect the rat hole.

Inside, she thought she saw movement.

Without thinking, she reached in. She had been bitten many times, not by rodents, but by Tad. The prospect of a rat bite didn't strike much fear into her, even knowing the damage this particular rat had done to her son. It would have to get through a lot of scars and gristle to do the same to her.

Elbow deep in the hole, she tapped her fingertips across the cold concrete floor. The sound coming from inside was less the quick skittering of tiny claws and more of a dragging. Something was definitely in there, and the prospect of grabbing it and ending this whole ordeal excited her. She could feel her heart beating. Her fingers found wetness. She pulled her hand out coated in red liquid. Blood?

She reached back in, fast this time, hoping to catch her prey off guard. She did. She caught a fistful of fur, latched onto it tight and quickly pulled it out of the hole. "Gotcha, you piece of shit!"

When the light revealed what she had withdrawn, she didn't do the natural thing. She didn't throw it to the floor. She didn't scream. She couldn't. It was as if the recording of her life hit a scratch and no matter how badly she wanted to move past that moment, it just stuck there. From her fist dangled the head of the exterminator, eyeholes filled with shit. The watery feces dripped down scratched cheeks. A single triumphant maggot erupted from amidst untamed nostril hair, appearing for only a moment before retreating back to its feast.

The sound of footsteps on the wooden stairs pulled her to her feet. She finally let the head drop when she heard Tad scream, "Amal, Momma!"

She turned and her son charged into her arms.

Something had followed him, lurching slowly down the steps. It wasn't a rat. If she had any way of foreseeing this, she would have prayed to God to send her a thousand rats, massive rats rife with rabies and plague – anything instead of this.

She held Tad tight.

The doctors of hell had sculpted this creature's body out of the tumors of the damned. Wisps of fur grew out of the endless lumps that riddled its body. Every inch of it oozed. Even its black eyes seemed to leak out of its face, reaching for Janie as its knotted legs carried it closer. Its clawed feet plodded tentatively, one step at a time. Mobility wasn't its strong suit, but that didn't make Janie any less frightened. From between its hind legs, it pissed black blood, leaving a trail on the steps behind it.

She backed up, still holding Tad, and heard something behind her, a distant sound, coming from the hole in the cinder blocks. This creature was not alone. More were on their way, coming from far beyond her basement walls.

The creature on the steps moved forward. Through a fissure in its gnarled snout, it bared its teeth at Janie and her fear gave way to a surprising thought: She could jump over this one. It wasn't much bigger than a cat, and it moved slowly. She could jump over it, slam the door and lock it in the basement. She could do it.

But could Tad?

Of course not. She would have to leave him and hurry back with a baseball bat to crush that thing's head in before it finished what it had started by eating Tad's thumb. She couldn't let it get her Taddy. She would come back for him. She always did. She had to. She was his mom. That's what moms did, no matter how hard, no matter how exhausting.

"You stay right here, Taddy," she ordered.

He nodded, shifting his weight frantically from foot to foot.

As the creature neared the last few steps, it hissed at her so hard froth formed on its boil-besotted lower lip. She ran as fast as her middle-aged legs would go and sprang up off the first step.

The creature reared, snagging her left ankle with its ragged talons as she soared over it. This sent her falling face first into the steps above it. Her nose burst and darkness twinkled around her, but she fought for consciousness as the creature toyed with the hole it had made in her jeans, trying to find flesh to dig into with those jagged, curved teeth – teeth that emerged from its mouth like tickling fingers as it got closer to its desire. Kicking only seemed to excite it. It clung tight.

"Amal!" Tad wailed from the bottom of the steps.

She looked down with horror to see Tad holding the exterminator's head over his, shaking as he shuffled closer to the staircase.

"Amal!" he wailed again. That wasn't fear in his voice. It was anger.

The creature turned, as if realizing it was being challenged.

No pitcher's mound had seen the likes of Tad's wind-up. His hurling arm and upper body reeled back, as if being sucked into a giant vacuum, while his left leg kicked forward like a puppet's on a string. Despite this awkward movement, the actual act of throwing turned suddenly graceful, and the head flew out of his hand at the perfect trajectory to smash the creature right between its eyes.

When struck, the creature unraveled itself from Janie. Finding a new target, it rushed toward Tad with a burst of speed, spurts of retched waste shooting from its backside as it ran. Tad didn't even try to escape. The creature latched onto Tad's legs and pulled them out from under him, dragging him toward the hole in the wall and whatever hid in the darkness beyond.

Before Janie could move, before she could grasp that her son, who could barely eat without her help, had saved her life, the creature's pustule ridden body vanished with Tad's feet into the darkness. Then his legs disappeared up to the ankles, up to the knees, up to the waist. The scrawny boy slid through the hole easily, only catching when he put his arms out against the wall, staring desperately at Janie.

"Momma?"

Blood pouring from her busted nose, Janie jumped down the steps and flung her body toward her son, catching his hand just in time.

She strained not only at the weight of that creature and her son, but at the weight of the 26 years of her life she had set aside to make him as comfortable as possible, to serve him, to put him first.

This was it, she realized. This was her opportunity to just let go, to just let him go and live her life. He stared at her with eyes bright and gray, eyes that saw only her, only her ever, nobody else, and never would. She was his world and he had become hers. But she wanted so much more. She had never been able to let go before. She had been strong – so strong – but that strength left her now. She felt her grip loosening as the creature pulled and growled a growl that crumbled every ounce of hardened courage she had left.

And after 26 years, Janie finally let go.

NIGHT GAMES

BY JOHN BODEN

They make no sound as they slink through the park. Shadows snaking around buildings and over or under fences. Phantoms in Keds and sweatshirts. They circle the stage area, by the outhouses and pause. The old man sleeps here, beneath the arbor by the side park entrance. His drunken snoring sounds like chainsaw buzz. The stars glitter in the sky and the long shadows surround him. He stirs once and settles back into his slumber. There is a small bubble nesting in the corner of his scabrous mouth. It grows and grows and then shrinks with his sour breaths.

Four small children, wearing plastic animal masks, stand in a semi-circle at his feet. The animal masks look ghastly in the moonlight; Piggy, Bunny, Kitty Kat and Ducky.

Piggy looks down and his breath condenses on the inside of his mask, nearly suffocating him with the stench of Cheerios and root beer. He sticks out his tongue and licks the moisture.

Ducky pours the gasoline while Kitty Kat lights the match. A hellish hiss and a sulfuric whiff of Hell and it dances from her tiny fingertips. A fiery-headed fairy diving toward damnation.

Bunny scampers back against the wall, the other three are her echoes. The old man manages one ragged scream before the flames melt his voice box. His coarse and wild beard blooms into a smoldering aura of fire and sizzling flesh. His rheumy eyes pop and sizzle and run like eggs. The flames dance in a combat orange reflection on the sheen of the masks the children wear. The stinking smoke climbs the night sky like a spectral ladder.

In less than an hour, the flames have died, and the man is still. His ragged clothing has melded with his flesh. He glistens wetly in the moonlight. Loking very much like a hog at one of the pig roasts they have in the park every Summer. Bunny hops forward and hunches herself. The hem of her pink dress touches his thigh and absorbs sickly pink moisture from the body. She reaches out and grasps his left hand. Dexterous digits are now charcoal and bone, she snaps off a pinky and a thumb. She stands and scurries back to the wall. "Go" she chirps.

Ducky and Kitty Kat hold hands as the saunter to the smoking corpse. Kitty pulls his tongue from the skull, it stretches cartoonishly and finally snaps free. She stuffs it into her sweatshirt pocket and points to Ducky. The boy kneels and takes a bite of the dead mans ear. It crunches like his grandma's fried chicken. He chews and swallows and takes another bite.

When they return to the wall, Piggy takes his turn. He undoes his trousers as he approaches. The dead man hisses and steams as the piss hits the ruins of his face.

• • •

The church is hot and the sermon long. Darren and Jeff sit near the back. Jeff dozing lightly, as Darren contemplates the spiritual ramifications of cutting a fart in the house of God. He looks at his grandmother and she shoots him a stern look that makes him rethink his urge. His stomach growls and she shakes her head. The Reverend goes on and on and on. Marcy sits beside her father, she fingers the hem of her dress, she is impressed she has gotten the stain out.

She looks up to front row and sees Becky sitting next her mother. She is thinking about her ballerina music box and the dead man's fingers that now live inside it. Her raven hair glistens and flutters in the breeze of the ceiling fans. While the Preacher thinks about their souls and salvation. Their parents think about working and bills and survival. The children think about next Friday night, and what the game might be. Becky had suggested they switch masks this week. Darren likes this idea. Darren agrees with anything the girls say.

Marcy was worried she'll get the Piggy mask. She grimaces at the recollection of Jeff licking the inside of his mask, disgusted. Boys were gross. They all stand and the organist introduces the hymn.

THE BREATH

BY JESSIE VOLK

Grown men don't fear the dark and they aren't afraid of closets. So ask yourself - are you going to live in fear like a pussy? Because this is your closet. It's your life. You can hear the world laughing in your head. And they're right, aren't they? A grown man afraid of a closet. Pathetic.

Without thinking, you punch the wall behind your head and the pain gives you a second wind. You leave the relative safety of your leather couch and grab a quart of crimson paint from the cupboard. Gripping the paintbrush like a dagger, you march over to the closet like it insulted your girl.

And the closet door snaps shut.

You only catch it out of the corner of your eye, but the sound is unmistakable. Goddamnit, you know you heard it, but now all you can hear is your blood pounding past your ears. It's all in your head. It's got to be in your head. Why is it so much harder to convince yourself in the middle of the night? You're seven years old again, hiding under the covers praying for the sunrise to hurry the fuck up.

A little time, a little distance. That's all you need. To build up the courage to check inside.

But you won't check inside.

• • •

The marketing position you landed in San Francisco was cause for celebration and you wanted an apartment to match your success. Something unique with lots of charm, vaulted ceilings, and a great view. You hired an agent and after a few misses she finds the perfect spot.

Two-car garage, roof deck, remodeled kitchen, plenty of room in the living room to fit your flat screen, all in the heart of Telegraph Hill. The place is perfect for you except for one thing. The centerpiece of the living room, the heart of this beautiful apartment, is a closet. It used to be a fireplace, explains the agent, before the last tenants installed the doors and bricked over the chimney.

"Technically it's an inglenook," she says offhandedly, "a sort of walk-in fireplace. There used to be benches inside so you could sit in with the fire."

The inglenook spills out of the apartment's northern wall, claiming a hefty chunk of the living room's floor plan. Like a call girl with oddly conservative dress, the solid oak doors shuttering the entrance simultaneously invites and shames your stares. Or maybe it's the carving sliced through the doors that draws you in. Two half circles arc across each door joining at the top and bottom to form a perfect ring, enveloping a set of nested squares three deep. Four gates on the top, bottom, left, and right connect the outer expanse with the inner sanctum, housing an eight pointed lotus at its center. In some spots, the carving dives an inch deep, in others it blends with the grain of the wood.

"Can the doors be removed?" you ask.

"You really have a thing against closet doors, huh?" says the agent. You have asked her this same question at each place she's shown you. "Once the place is yours you can do what you want, but they were carved specifically for this space. And they're gorgeous..."

Not a closet, you think. It's a fireplace.

"Nevermind. I'll take it."

● ● ●

The Breath. That's what you named it. It hid in closets and stalked you all your life, lashing out at the worst times. Like that time in freshman year, at one of Vicki Henson's keggers.

A girl at the party catches your eye. She isn't much of a look-er, didn't even catch her name, but she's friendly enough. Both of you are hammered, so what the hell? You bring her to one of the back bedrooms. It's a tiny guest bedroom with a flimsy closet door. The chick straddles you on the bed, nibbling on your ear-lobe with heavy sighs. But the Breath is louder, a wheezing that you try to block out of your beer-fogged mind.

The chick's bra is almost off when the closet door rattles. You lose your shit. Pants half undone, you bolt up and tear the closet door clean off its hinges. The girl grabs her blouse and bolts. She'll probably tell everyone at the party you're nuts. You hide in that back bedroom to sleep it off.

In the morning, you come out of your hiding spot to apolo-gize to Vicki about the door, blaming too much booze for the outburst. You go back with her to assess the damage and it hits you: you hadn't heard the Breath all night. Even now, silent. Not a sigh since you ripped the door clean off. No closet door means nothing to hide behind, nothing to slam. You mumble another apology to Vicki, and leave before she can make you fix it. You race home to dismantle your own closet door. Your parents raise an eyebrow or two, but they leave you alone. Life becomes so quiet you start to forget. You have finally outsmarted the thing hiding just beyond reach.

• • •

Before you move in to your new apartment on Telegraph Hill, you have the agent remove the doors from the rest of the closets. You stow your things in these neutered closets, but you leave the inglenook empty. You half consider using it once you finish unpacking, working up the courage to peek inside. It's about three feet deep, a walk-in closet. One of the stone benches is still accessible, but the other has been converted into storage, with half a dozen shelves neatly spaced up to the ceiling. The fireplace itself sits unused in the rear wall, ash stained firebricks the only clue to its former purpose. You tell yourself that there isn't anything left to store inside, but really it still makes you nervous. If you're honest with yourself, you look inside because you want to check that it's empty. And of course it is, but when you close the door you have this feeling... like you're the putz in a magic show nodding to the audience that the box is empty right before the turn.

The inglenook makes feng shuiing your new living room nearly impossible. You settle on hanging the flat screen on the opposite wall, but the cable guy isn't scheduled to come by for another week. You can get one or two digital channels with your antenna, but no ESPN, no Sportscenter. Everything else seems bland. Bored, you shut off the TV and pass the time surveying the inglenook doors instead. In your mind's eye, you stroke the seam where the two doors meet. They don't come together perfectly. There's a gap that gets wider at the top. Wide enough that someone inside could press their eye to the gap and peer out. Finding this imperfection, you relax. As though you've caught your foe in a moment of weakness. Tracing the carving you get lost, and pass out on the couch.

• • •

The Breath terrorized you more when you were younger. In middle school, it sent minions beyond its doors. Every closet served as a portal for the invasion, especially those at school. You tried your best to ignore them, but the strain of vigilance left you on edge.

There is one that finds you in art class. He waits in the corner dressed all in black. He's innocuous enough that he might not be from the closet except that no one else seems to notice him. Mr. Liddell tells the class to paint a scene from your summer vacation, but all you can manage is black on black. You feel the man in black move closer, standing right behind you, his breath...

the Breath at your neck. You throw an elbow behind your head and to your surprise you connect with something solid. He goes down, taking a few easels and paint brushes to the linoleum with him. But it's Mr. Liddell. The man in black has vanished.

The counselor sends you home with a note for your parents. Assaulting a teacher. Aggressive demeanor. Disturbing behavior. Disciplinary action. Possible suspension. You hide the note, but the school calls anyway. Your parents are cross and any attempt to explain the mix up, about the man in black, gets you nowhere but grounded.

That night you take the note and the black on black painting and crumple them in a waste bin in the closet. You light everything on fire with one of those handheld lighters from the kitchen. You can hear the Breath sniffing the smoke in the shadows. The bits of paper become light in a moment of metamorphosis, but it's too short lived. To fight off the darkness, you add some newspaper, then more. Then you take the lighter to other things and soon the whole closet is as bright as the sun. The crackle of the flames drowns out the sound of the Breath and you smile.

Afterwards, you promise Dr. Patel and your parents no more fire, but you keep a book of matches under your mattress just in case. Because after the fire, the invasion stops, the Breath's minions are gone. You fought back and now they know you're no easy prey.

● ● ●

The notion to paint the inglenook doors comes to you all at once. Color to the grain would make the carving pop. Make it your own.

If you're going to do it, you want it to be tasteful. A quick search on the internet pegs the carving as a 'mandala', some hocus pocus symbol for the universe. It seems fairly authentic, could have easily been imported, which raises the stakes. Don't want to ruin this gem by scribbling on it like a kid with a broken crayon. You read, you plan, you research, looking up color pairings in your spare time, reading through painting how-to's on your lunch break, doodling mandalas through meetings. You even consider a trip to Tibet to see one in person. The cable guy comes and goes, but the TV stays cold. A month goes by and you can't wait any longer. You leave work early and buy brushes and paint. You choose your colors and start adding a few brush strokes to mark what will go where. Easy. Almost paint by number.

At first it's soothing. It becomes your favorite spot in the house. You can't wait to get home to work on your new obsession. But it's slow going. You paint a small part of it and it looks good, but you get too excited. Afraid if you continue, the paint on the door won't match what's in your head. But each little bit makes it more real - takes you closer to your masterpiece.

● ● ●

Before little league practice, the team would always congregate around this shed behind the dugout. It was an old wooden box where they'd store the extra bases and the tee, but for some unknown reason, this rotting box was always the meeting place.

It's in this box that you learn that the Breath isn't confined to the closet in your bedroom.

Rodney's the team bully. Twice as big as any of the other 10-year-olds, he likes to push around the smaller kids, with a smirk that slices across his freckled face. His newest game is running headlong into the shed with a batting helmet on and daring other kids to do the same. Today it's your turn, so he asks you to get helmets from the shed.

Two steps inside the door and you've already grabbed a helmet. You're about to leave but something stops you. Seething in hot dust in the back corner, you hear it. In the patch of light from the open door, a daddy longlegs skitters across the soft wood floor. Rodney slams the door behind you, trapping you inside.

Enveloped in darkness, you can feel hundreds of spiders, their delicate legs alighting on your shoes, crawling up your pant legs, falling on your head and shoulders. You slam against the door, screaming whatever you can, pleas, curses, anything to get the door open. You can feel them under your shirt, over your eyes, scratching at your ears, flowing in to your mouth to muffle your screams. Suffocating you in the dark.

The door pops open and you stumble out, still clinging to the helmet. You brush off the rest of the spiders and, as you scramble off the ground, you realize you've pissed yourself. Yellow stains on your white trousers.

"Oh my god! Did the baby wet himself?" laughs Rodney. Some of the other boys join in; some of them avoid your eyes in pity. Rodney shakes with laughter so hard he can barely keep on his feet. You snap and hurl the helmet at him. Rodney swats it away, but you use the distraction to punch him straight in the gut. He keels over to the ground and you start kicking. Cleats pounding dust into his forearms and knees as the little bitch tries to roll away. You don't stop until your mother pulls you away, rushing you to the car where you sit, blinded by tears and adrenaline.

● ● ●

It happens while you're painting the north gate. It's a Monday night after work, alone in your apartment. You have finished the other three gates in the carving, and now you've moved to the one at the top that's split in two by the crack in the doors. You are painting it white. As you work, your nose whistles. You rub your nostrils across the back of your hand a few times to get rid of the sound. No dice. You try your best to ignore it.

Then the door rattles.

It startles you so much your hand shakes and you drop your brush. It takes you a second to calm down. Could have easily bumped it with your foot, you tell yourself. There's nothing in there, dummy. It's not even a closet.

Then you realize you can still hear that nose whistle even though you're holding your breath. That's enough painting for tonight.

But the heaviness remains the next day. The inglenook pulls and repels you like waves in the ocean. Get home from work, time you normally reserve for working on your masterpiece, and you pace for a good half an hour working up the courage to approach your own closet.

Every night you build up the courage, and every night it's terrifying. You swear you can hear the Breath inside, seething through the crack in the door. The boogeyman resurrected. Shuffling around inside. The pounding in your chest, the choking breaths. Swells of awfulness, rolling through the moment and dragging you under. You're losing your mind. That has to be it. There's nothing in the closet, there's no rattle, you're losing it. But you won't check. You never check. Either you open it to find all the horrors of your childhood or you open an empty closet. Which is worse?

• • •

The memory of how it all started is lost in your childhood. The Breath has been there from the beginning, waiting inside your closet. The closet doors have always been a thinly guarded border to a hostile territory. Your enemies wait in the night, amassing at the gate. The witching hour would be the perfect time for a bloody annexation of your bedroom. Some nights it rages, rattling the door in its frame, other nights are quiet and you have to strain to hear it seething through the wooden slats. Some nights you can feel it exhale across your face hot and dense. At some point, maybe when you are six or seven, the comforting tone in your parents' voices adopts an edge of annoyance. You learn to be ashamed of your fear. You stop asking mother to check the closet. You nod when father tells you it's all in your head. Even though your eyes are blood shot from hours of listening and feigning sleep.

You use rituals to protect yourself. Closet light on and off three times. Tap the door knob five times. Lay your socks on the edge of the bed as a decoy. Close your eyes and keep them closed all night, no matter what you hear.

• • •

The carving is half finished and you wish you had never started. You could still have the doors removed, but you can't bring yourself to do it. They're too beautiful now, too consuming. You curse under your breath, your hands straining to hold the brush steady. Why can't you stop?

The door breathes open.

You fall backward to the floor. This was no accident. The right door is open a clean foot, no way that happened on its own. On the door you had been painting, you see a large smudge of blue paint beyond the north gate on one of the outer walls. You must have pushed against the door with your brush in your leap backwards. At the rate you've been going, it will take you weeks to fix the damage.

Enough. No more! Whatever's in the closet, whatever's been tormenting you, it's time to drag it out.

Stepping inside the closet, you're immediately disoriented. It's bigger than you remember, or maybe you're smaller. The ceiling must be 20 feet high and decorated with mandala carvings you hadn't noticed before. The back of the closet is a vanishing point steeped in a thick curtain of darkness. The shelving over the left bench is gone. In its place sits a thing. You recognize him instantly despite the dark. Despite not being able to focus on his face.

He gestures for you to sit on the opposite bench. Between you burns a blue fire on the floor. Weird, you think, the Breath hates fire.

"Surprised to see me in here, aren't you?" you ask.

"Surprised... to see... you?" He speaks as if he's asleep, though he sits tall and alert.

"Yeah, I walked right in here. That bullshit doesn't work on me. I'm not a child anymore."

"No. Not a child anymore."

"What, am I talking to a fucking echo? Leave! Or I swear to God, I'll burn this place to the ground!"

"Burn? This place?"

"Yeah. You and your whole army," you say, pointing to the impossibly infinite hallway.

"No. Not mine. Those nightmares are in your mind. They were always in your mind."

"Screw you. An entire childhood of torment... all in my head."

"Yes. The war is in your mind. You battle yourself for no reason. Even this. Why do we do this?"

"Why... what? You do this! I just wanted to paint!"

"Yes, please paint. It brings you peace."

Wait, what's the angle? It wants you to paint? It doesn't make sense. Is this even the Breath? It has to be, but you're not afraid. You try to focus on its face, but the features are in a blur.

"Get out," you insist. "Get out or I'll torch this place!"

"Please, no more war," he says in a wavering voice. "Not again. I'm not your enemy."

You know it's lying. The rage is so sweet you let it roll over you like a warm blanket. You leap past the blue flame and attack. Two hands wrapped around its neck, you start to choke him. Choke the life out of a face that's so familiar. So familiar because... because it's your face. This is your face. Your neck between your hands. Your crushed windpipe.

"Please," says the Breath, "I don't want to be the villain anymore."

And then the scene reverses. Instead of you choking him, you switch perspectives. Now you are him, and he is you. You feel the room swim and your vision blurs. But you don't pass out. He lets you go and you see him leave through the closet door. Shutting you inside your box. Now you are the monster in the closet. You always were.

HUNGRY

BY ED KURTZ

Despite having spent an entire childhood hanging his head in shame and loneliness due to a lifetime of fatness, a growth spurt the summer of his fourteenth birthday had blessed Lionel with an altogether new body. It was as though God heard his prayer and fulfilled his most earnest wish—almost overnight, he was tall and thin and even more than a little handsome. That autumn Lionel commenced his high school career with a confidence he never knew was possible. He held his head high in the hallways for the first time, and the other kids took notice. His old junior high buddies were confused, his former antagonists were impressed, and several fresh young girls recognized his existence as though they had never seen him before, which they probably had not.

It was like a dream; the best damn dream Lionel ever had. By the second semester of his freshman year, he scored a lead role in the school play—Mortimer in *Arsenic and Old Lace*—and actually turned the coach down when he asked Lionel to try out for the basketball team. He might not have been fat anymore, but he still loathed sports and just about anyone who participated in them. Thinness did not change everything.

One thing it did change, however, was his relationship to the opposite sex. Just a year earlier, a blink of the eye on a cosmic scale, the only response he could ever elicit from a girl was laughter or contempt. Now they smiled at him. Genuine, entirely non-ironic smiles that conveyed interest in who he was and what he might come to think of them. Initially he played it cool. He maintained a veneer of indifference, a mask to conceal his persistent shyness. But that was before the party that followed the final performance of the play where Jacquie Koegler, Elaine to his Mortimer, dragged him into the garage for a half-hour make-out session. Looking back, Lionel would come to consider that the spark that lit the fuse.

Lionel and Jacquie had a thing for a while, a sort of hand-holding, necking, over the clothes foreplay kind of thing, but that came crashing down toward the end of summer. The longer these little private games went on, the more he wanted to advance them to the next level. Squeezing her small, pointy breasts through both sweater and bra had been nice at the beginning, but it grew tiresome, stale. There was more they could be doing. Much more. And the more insistent he became about it, the more distressed Jacquie became in response. She wanted to wait until she was eighteen. He did not want to wait another day.

So he didn't. When she showed up unannounced on his sixteenth birthday at his parents' front door, he told her to get back in her little hatchback and go the fuck away. Jacquie left in tears and Lionel began his systematic search for the easiest girls in school. Sarah was the first: an awkward, sweaty fumbling that took place in the backseat of her father's station wagon. Lionel was so excited about it that he told nearly everyone in school the following term. Her reputation irreversibly ruined, Sarah transferred to another school district and Lionel never heard from her again. He never thought about her, either. By then he had gone from Jennifer to Tara to Candace, back to Tara and onto Emily, Sophie, and that red-haired girl from Delaware whose name he could not recall. (Maggie? Megan?) He grew more daring and pushy with each new experience, aware of the fact that for every girl who said *No* there were four more out there that were bound to say *Yes*.

He had no shame. Wouldn't have wanted any were a choice given.

Adolescence was glorious for Lionel. Whatever lay beyond that was the most inconsequential thing in the universe. All that mattered to him was the next lay, and whether or not he was going to experience something new and audacious, maybe even something no one had ever tried before, though his teenaged imagination had its limits.

He grew his hair long and pierced his ears. He acted disaffected and hip as hell and started smoking. He never had another girlfriend after Jacquie because commitment was nowhere when there were a thousand girls out there he had not yet tried.

Lionel turned eighteen the summer after graduation. Most of the kids he knew moved away, went to college, joined the service. The rest of them stuck around and took low-paying jobs, got apartments. A few went and got hitched, shotgun weddings usually. But Lionel stayed at home, unemployed and disaffected in a very real way for the first time in his short life. Adolescence was at its twilight, a harsh reality he could do nothing about, and he turned decidedly bitter about it. So he whittled the next year away in his room, alternately watching cable TV and reading dogeared paperbacks. And he ate.

He ate a lot.

● ● ●

Corn chips with cheese dip, chocolate Ding-a-Lings, soda pop and beer. Ice cream when his mother brought it home from the supermarket, which was about once a week. He made sundaes replete with peanuts, chocolate chips, chocolate syrup, and a ring of cookies around the three densely packed scoops in the bowl. Double layer nachos were another favorite, whereby he arranged a layer of corn chips on a serving plate, topped it with cheese and hamburger meat and jalapeños, and then repeated the process for a second story. He ate hot dogs three and four at a time and never got going in the morning until he had a full breakfast of fried eggs, bacon, hash browns with ketchup, and heavily buttered toast.

Lionel ate and he drank and he smoked. Occasionally the telephone would ring, and on rare occasion he assented to a visit from some old acquaintance, provided that they did not cramp his style and brought their own chow. Once, around Christmas, Tara called him up. She said she had been thinking about him and wondered what he was up to. She was preparing to move to Los Angeles, she said, and thought it would be nice to see Lionel before she left. It might have been an opportunity, perhaps even an invitation, but one look at the tower of Polish sausages on the plate in front of him was enough to convince Lionel that he did not desire any companionship. He wished her a nice life and hung up the phone. After he finished off the sausages, he devoured a heaping sundae before waddling out to the back porch for a smoke. He fell asleep with the third cigarette in a row burning down to the filter in the ashtray.

• • •

At the end of his first year of legal adulthood, Lionel's mother kicked him out of the house. He bummed around friends' couches for a few weeks, but then the money ran out and he was hungry. Being essentially homeless was one thing, but missing meals was something else altogether. So he took the first job he was offered, became a desk clerk at the interstate motel on the west side of town, and two weeks after that he had his own place.

It was a crummy place, small and dirty and infested with cockroaches, but Lionel did not mind. It was a place to sleep. He spent most of his waking hours behind the front desk of the motel, anyway. Which was where he met Carla.

She was tall and lean, her skin brown like tea and her eyes big and inviting. The first time he saw her, she was following a middle-aged ne'er-do-well in a mesh trucker hat (TAKE THIS JOB AND SHOVE IT, it read) to the elevator, sashaying as she turned to wink at Lionel before the steel doors slid shut. He was not stupid—he knew what she was about and he expected he would see her again.

As it happened, he saw Carla quite a lot after that, two or three times a week. She always gave him a wink on her way to the elevator. Eventually, some four or five weeks into the gig, she stopped at the front desk after her john went on his way. She wore pink leggings under a pair of tight cut-offs and an open back halter top that clung to her massive fake breasts. Nice, but not quite enough to sustain Lionel's attention when there was a double bacon cheeseburger and a translucent bag of French fries dripping grease in front of him.

"I'm Carla," she said between gum-smacks.

"I know."

The girl smiled wryly and spit her gum out into her hand.

"Yeah? How you know that?"

"Javier told me."

Javier was the night janitor and, according to him, an occasional client of Carla's. Upon hearing his name, she gave a short laugh.

"Javier," she said. "That fucking guy."

Lionel nodded and stuffed a handful of fries into his mouth.

"At fuh'ing 'uy," he agreed.

Carla arched one well-plucked eyebrow and smiled from one side of her mouth.

"You can sure pack away some food, huh?"

Lionel swallowed hard and narrowed his eyes at her. A hundred nasty retorts flooded through his mind but he did not utter any of them. He only stared daggers at her until she took the hint and slunk off.

• • •

Food was fast developing into a problem for Lionel. Things that used to taste wonderful were losing their thrall. Worse still: even the heartiest, fattiest foods failed to sate his demanding hunger. He was unabashed in devouring six prepackaged frozen dinners over the course of a single night shift, refusing to pay any mind to Javier's astonishment at his persistent appetite and persistently expanding torso. The following night he ate seven of them. He had to force himself to repress his gag reflex, choking back barbequed chicken medallions and apple cobblers and one cheese covered potato spear after another. They all tasted like cardboard marinated on a public men's room floor, but he swallowed every bite. All to no avail.

Lionel was still hungry.

• • •

Carla winked, glided into the elevator and went up for a session with a sour faced black kid who looked more afraid than tough. An hour later the kid went through the lobby with his hands stuffed in his pockets, doing everything in his power to avoid eye contact with the fat night porter. A moment after that, Carla appeared in front of Lionel, her blonde-tipped brown hair a shambles and her make-up smeared all over her face like a Jackson Pollack.

She was loaded.

Lionel shifted uncomfortably in his chair, plunged his hand into an economy sized bag of cheese doodles, and watched Carla sway back and forth as he shoved the orange-powdered curls in his mouth.

"You wanta go?" she slurred.

"Go where?"

"Upstairs, dummy." She cupped her small hands under her breasts and heaved them up. "You want summa this, fat boy?"

Lionel ducked his head like a disapproving parent.

"I'm not paying you for sex," he said.

He meant it. Ever since high school Lionel had gradually lost all interest in sex. It was not guilt; he did not feel one iota of pity for the girls he'd duped into bed during his magnificent teenage years. He simply could not be bothered with that sort of thing anymore. It did not satisfy him.

"Who's paying?" Carla said, a little too loudly. "C'mon up. I'll show ya how's it done. On the house."

Lionel looked at her amplified cleavage, still hoisted up with her hands, and then back down to his orange stained fingers. The cheese doodles failed to satisfy him, too.

He plugged his thumb in his mouth and sucked the salty powder off, followed by the rest of his fingers, one by one. All the while he considered Carla's alcohol-fueled proposal. It had been a long time since last he'd laid a girl. A good two years and somewhere in the neighborhood of ninety-five pounds ago. Lionel could almost hear his dead father's voice, upbraiding him from beyond the grave: *You aren't* queer, *are you?*

He wiped his slimy fingers off on his slacks and scooted back in the chair. Carla smiled, but it looked more like a sneer. She gestured with her hand and cooed, "Come on, then."

Lionel got up and quietly followed her across the lobby to the elevator.

• • •

In the nine weeks since he began working at the motel, Lionel had never once set foot in any of its twenty-four rooms. He had no reason to—Javier and Maria cleaned them up and there was a contracted, on-call maintenance guy for when the toilets overflowed or the water wouldn't come on. The only thing they paid Lionel for was checking the rooms out and maintaining some semblance of order in the lobby and front parking lot. Mostly he just ate and tried not to nod off. Once or twice he'd brought some porn up on the internet, but predictably he attained no pleasure from it.

Carla always used the same room, number 24 on the second story at the end of the hall. She had her own key and Lionel never gave it to anyone else. It was an arrangement between her and the boss; Lionel just sort of got sucked into it. Now, standing in the doorway to the infamously licentious room, he considered that arrangement and what perks the boss doubtlessly reaped from it. That, in turn, led him to wonder if the boss had in fact *instructed* Carla to play this stupid reprobate game. *Give the lardass a whirl, it'll thrill his huge pants off.*

The notion sent shockwaves of hot anger through his body. As far as he was concerned, he refrained from sex because he was uninterested, not because he was fat and, possibly, unattractive to the opposite sex—much less *incapable*. That anyone would ambush him like this and consider it a kindness was enough to make him scream.

He did not scream. He merely shut the door, latched the guard chain and stood there in silence to see what happened next. Carla smiled lamely and staggered over to the unmade bed. Javier and Maria never entered that particular room. Cleaning it up was entirely up to Carla. The air was musky, sweaty-smelling.

"C'mon," she said, patting the bed with one hand while fumbling with the buttons on her cut-offs with the other. "Siddown."

Lionel did as he was told. The thin, soiled mattress creaked noisily beneath his tremendous weight. The girl wiggled her hips until the cut-offs dropped down to her ankles, stepped out of them and then started working on her halter top. Lionel had never seen anyone have this much trouble getting undressed.

"Aren't you gunna get your clothes off?" she asked.

"It's a little cold in here."

"I'll warm you up."

"There's a lot of me to warm up and not a lot of you to do it."

Carla screwed up her face, trying to process what he'd said.

"I mean I'm fat," he explained.

"I don't mind. I've fucked fat guys. I just do it on top, you know?"

She laughed a little at that, but Lionel did not find it particularly funny. When Carla finally got her bra unhooked, she made a diving stance with her arms and let slide right off. He frowned at her naked breasts. They stood at permanent attention and he reckoned that they were too far apart and looked like she had stuffed a couple of softballs into them.

"You like em?" she asked.

He shrugged indifferently.

"Five thousand bucks I got here," she said, once again hoisting them with her hands. Her pride and joy. Lionel could think of a lot of better ways to spend five grand.

"That's a lot," he said.

"Still payin' it off, but that's what this place is for, right?"

"I guess so."

"Get outta your clothes, now. Let's get to it."

She sloughed off her panties and performed an awkward tiger crawl across the bed to him, fighting to keep her balance all the way. Her tits did not sway at all. Lionel sighed. He wished he never followed her up there in the first place. All the same, he did as she asked and pulled his shirt up over his head.

"Attaboy," Carla cooed.

He unbuckled his belt, unbuttoned his doodle-streaked trousers, let them fall to the floor. She kneeled beside him on the bed, rubbing her cold, dry hands all over his flabby, pale torso and making weird moaning sounds that were anything but alluring. The only thing about her that he liked was her perfume, but she wore too much of it.

"Boxers, too," she admonished him.

He obeyed, bending over with some difficulty to push his underwear down. Now they were both stark naked, he and Carla— her with the bad boob job and him with the small, flaccid penis he could not see for his own massive stomach. He sighed again, wondering what had possessed him to come up there when he knew damn well what he was in for. Shame and disappointment.

His stomach growled.

It got worse from there. Carla reached out with both hands and began fumbling with Lionel's cock, tugging and rubbing and rolling it around like she was trying to make a worm out of clay. The muscles in his stomach and shoulders tensed up and he knitted his brow. A minute or two later she released him and gazed at his penis with bewilderment.

"Nothing?" she said.

That's about the size of it, Lionel thought. Nothing at all.

His stomach rumbled some more, cramped a bit.

Carla leaned back against the headboard and frowned. She

was still glaring at his limp member like it was some complex puzzle that needed figuring out. Lionel felt like crying. All he wanted now was to get out of room 24 as quickly as possible and go find something to eat. Something good, something that might finally stave off the hunger. He thought that maybe if he was not so goddamned hungry then something might have happened between him and Carla.

He reached down, grabbed his boxers by the gradually weakening elastic and pulled them back up to his waist. Carla let out a snort.

"I'm going to get back to work," he said lamely.

"Yeah," she said. She was sobering up now, her face a mask of dejection and humiliation. "You do that."

• • •

He lay awake most of the morning, listening to the cockroaches skitter inside the walls and worrying about the pain in his abdomen. When he'd gotten back to his apartment around six AM, he made two hoagie sandwiches with provolone, pepperoni, salami, mustard, mayonnaise. They tasted like the back of a postage stamp and left him hungrier than ever. Around nine he started to cry. Lionel didn't know what he was going to do.

• • •

The lobby phone rang at a quarter to midnight. The LED readout on the little gray screen informed Lionel that the call was coming from room 24. He groaned and stared at the phone, waiting for it stop ringing. It didn't. He picked up on the fourteenth ring.

"I need help," Carla weakly complained. "Can you come up here, please?"

"Kinda busy," he lied.

"It's serious," she said. "Please come when you can."

Lionel grumbled and cursed under his breath. (*Fuck, fuck, fuck*) But he went up anyway.

She was bent over on the edge of the bed, sobbing into her hands. The room smelled musty and astringent, like sweat and liquor. It was only when Lionel sat down on the mattress beside her that he realized that Carla had been cut up pretty badly. A dozen or more seeping red lines adorned her arms, her neck and her face. Gently, he took her left arm and turned it over. Her palm was split open, too. She had tried to defend herself and got slashed for her trouble. He made a clicking noise with his tongue.

"Is he gone?"

She nodded. Her face was a mess of streaked mascara and tears and blood.

"You want me to call the police?"

"No," she said, softly. "They won't do anything. Not for me."

Lionel frowned, decided that she was probably right. People who got hurt during the commission of a crime did not tend to elicit much sympathy from cops.

With a heavy sigh he lifted himself up, toddled over to the bathroom, and ran cold water over a washcloth. He then returned to Carla's side and dabbed at her wounds, washing the dried blood away. She winced. And the wounds started to bleed anew.

"There's a first aid kit in the office," he said. "Take me five minutes to go get it and come back."

He started to rise, but Carla tugged at his sleeve to bring him back down.

"No, not yet. Please just sit here a minute."

"Got to stop that bleeding."

"I know. But just a minute. I won't bleed to death or anything."

He sat back down and looked at her. She did not look back. He felt awkward, he didn't know what to say. He wanted to ask who the guy was and what set him off, maybe he was just a psycho who liked to cut women up, but he kept his mouth shut. There wasn't any benefit in analyzing the thing right then and there. She just needed the company, he reckoned.

Wrapping his heavy arm around her back, he drew her small body into him. She buried her face in his chest, cried a little more and, after they flattened out on the bed, she fell asleep. He listened to her breath in and out for a while, and it turned out to be the first thing to successfully lull him to sleep in a long, long time.

• • •

The furious roaring of his stomach woke him up with a start. He glanced at the digital alarm clock on the nightstand and blinked until the glowing red numbers came into focus. Half past two in the morning and he was supposed to be at his desk. Not too many people came into the lobby at that hour on a Wednesday—or was it Thursday now? —but *still*.

Lionel sucked in a deep breath and stared at the yellow, banana-shaped water stain on the ceiling. He could have eaten fifty bananas and he knew he would still be hungry when he was done. This was not the first time it occurred to him that life had lost all its appeal, all of its rewards and pleasures. He was merely going through the motions at this point, like a cockroach that did not even know it was alive. It just did as it was programmed to do—eat, shit, sleep, breed. None of which enticed Lionel in the least.

He supposed the cockroach probably had a more gratifying existence than he did.

Carla shifted, moaned softly. She flung her arm over Lionel's expansive stomach and nuzzled her face into his neck. He shivered slightly as she kissed him, lightly, wondering if she was still asleep, if she was dreaming that she was with somebody else entirely. Someone thinner, more handsome; someone who could give her what she wanted. She moaned again and moved her hand up to his face, cradling his fleshy jowls with her soft, wounded palm.

He turned his head so that his lips brushed against her hand. His stomach growled again and his abdomen cramped. The prickly stubble on his face had scratched away some of the soft scab of the cut and it was beading up with bright red droplets.

He darted his tongue out and licked the blood.

His mouth watered at the sweet, metallic taste of it. Carla kissed him on the neck again, hard and lingering. The wound continued to well up and Lionel lapped it up over and over again. And the girl kept on kissing him, making loud smacking sounds and quiet, sensual groans.

"Are you awake?" he whispered.

Carla said, "Don't stop."

● ● ●

The day of Lionel's twentieth birthday he received an unexpected phone call from Tara. She wanted to wish him a happy birthday and see how he was doing and tell him all about the baby she just had with her new husband who was off in Korea with the Army. It was an awkward conversation but not at all unpleasant, and they were both sincere when they expressed well wishes and said goodbye. Lionel hung the phone up with a smile. Then he brushed his teeth and got dressed and went in to work.

He did not much mind working on his birthday, although his shift started at midnight so he guessed it was not technically his birthday anymore, anyway. It was a slow night, only three check-ins, none of them remarkable in any way. Just a few weary travelers stopping over on their way to wherever. By four A.M. Lionel had not seen another human being in an hour and a half. The quiet was making him feel a bit lonely. The thundering in his massive belly, larger than ever before, reminded him that he was hungry, too.

Fortunately for Lionel, there was a single solution to both problems.

He got up, rounded the front desk, and headed for the elevator. He rode up the second floor, walked down to the end of the hallway, and shoved his master key into the lock at room 24.

Carla sat in the wingback chair by the heating unit, smoking a cigarette and waiting patiently for him. A broad smile spread across her face when he came into the room. The scars on her face had healed quite nicely; Lionel could barely see them anymore without looking closely. She was radiant. Beautiful. He returned the smile as he shut and locked the door.

She did not get up to hug him—she'd already unstrapped the prosthetic leg and leaned it up against the bed. It got a bit uncomfortable after a while, so she liked to keep it off when she did not need it. The tissue around the stump, about four inches above where her knee used to be, was not as smooth and colorless as some of her other scar tissue, but that was only because Lionel was not quite finished with it yet. There was still good meat there, around her fleshy thigh, before he would get to work on her remaining leg.

He crossed the room and leaned down for a kiss. She pressed her full lips tightly against his and they kissed deeply for a while. He ran his thick fingers through her hair while their tongues met and mutually explored, exposing the gnarled strip on the left side of her head where there used to be an ear. Lionel had eaten it raw, cartilage and all. Carla reached around and touched him with a three-fingered hand. He had taken the ring and pinky fingers at her request, leaving her enough dexterity with which to operate on a relatively normal basis. He gently kissed the tips of her remaining digits, playfully snapping his teeth at them as though he meant to bite them off. She giggled and gave him a teasing shove.

"I missed you," she said.

"I love you," he replied. "My little sweet-meat."

Lionel then lifted her up and carried her over to the bed. He undressed her, slowly and sensually, taking his time. And he then undressed himself. They made love, he and Carla, moving in rhythmic harmony with one another, climaxing at the same time.

When they were done, Lionel took a hot shower while Carla waited on the bed and smoked another cigarette. Steam rose from his naked body in curling wisps as he came back into the room, toweling off. Carla was beaming, her big brown eyes taking him all in, loving him wholly. Stubbing her cigarette out in the ashtray with one hand, she held up the rubber tourniquet in the other. His knife gleamed on top of the comforter beside her, clean and ready.

"Are you hungry, baby?" she purred.

Lionel grinned, nodded, and went to work.

MEAT DISTRICT

BY LUCAS MANGUM

Stacia dropped the dusty cardboard box on the floor of her bare apartment. The words, "Meat District," were printed in capital letters on one side. Outside her window the city rumbled and roared, a beast that never slept. She surveyed the box's peeling strips of packing tape and collapsed corners from decades of rough handling, and tried to imagine what contents were sealed within.

She knew a little, but not everything. Her grandfather had published a comic in the late 1950s. It had a limited run before being banned, and most copies were lost, except for whatever remained in the box at her feet.

After the funeral she'd taken on the responsibility of archiving the works. She knew next to nothing about him, except that he'd been an outsider. Like her. Maybe in him she'd find something to which she could connect.

With his passing she'd realized how disconnected she actually was. She lived alone. She worked excessively, pouring her time into blogs and local newspaper articles. That left little time for friends or romantic involvement. And speaking to her family was out of the question.

Her grandfather had been dead a month, and it had taken her that long to work up the will to gather what few items he had left behind. The idea of reconnecting with anyone from her family, outsider like her or not, was a daunting thought.

Now, she could hardly bring herself to take inventory of his things. Tension assaulted her body as she touched the lid, making her feel like a reluctant Pandora.

She stepped away from the box and said, "Not yet."

She pushed it into the corner, went to the kitchen, and made dinner. She ate alone, a single candle the only light on the table. Soft jazz played through a sound system in a separate room. This was her evening ritual. It calmed her now even as she planned to look into her family's past.

When she finished eating, she smoked out on her balcony, procrastinating now, but telling herself that she needed to wait. She could open the box tomorrow after a good night's sleep, if she really wasn't yet comfortable. Would she ever be?

The city lights shined like stars in a black night sky. She shut her eyes and let her other senses overtake her. A powerful stink lingered in the air tonight, like algae or sewage, trapped by the humidity that hung thickly around her.

She let the cigarette burn down to the filter, tossed it over the balcony and watched it fall to the sidewalk seventeen stories below before reentering the apartment.

She'd scraped together the money from her freelance work to get the apartment three years ago. It was in the city in which she'd grown up. Even though her family still lived in the city and still played a huge part in the city's affairs, she'd never quite been able to leave, despite wanting nothing to do with them. It was as if the city, the life force that pulsed within it, pulsed within her, and if she would leave, she'd wither away to a lifeless husk.

From the corner, the box silently dared her to open it. She toyed with the idea of never opening it, of carrying it downstairs and throwing it into the dumpster. Or, she thought, even better; hurling it over her balcony so it would fall ten stories and burst upon impact, its contents scattering across the street to be ignored like so much rubbish.

Pulling her thoughts from the box, she sat down in front of the TV and aimlessly flipped through the stations before settling on an expose documentary on the farming industry.

Sleep claimed her and when she woke, it was into darkness.

She switched on a lamp and almost instinctually looked at the box. It sat beside the couch, visibly unremarkable, but the promise of mysteries within demanded reverence. She pulled it out, set it in the center of the room, and knelt before it.

The first issue rested on top of several others, along with photos, a plastic baggie full of old coins, and other knick knacks. Upon opening to the first page of the issue on top, near-paralyzing horror gripped her. The first panel was a full page spread of a gutted pig hanging from a meat hook. The entrails were piled in a steaming red heap on the floor below and within them human body parts were stuffed inside. Hands and feet that looked as if they'd been tenderized were mixed among the innards, alongside a severed head with its eyeballs scooped out and shattered ribcage.

She could see why the book had been challenged in its time. For the 1950s, this was graphic, groundbreaking stuff. And to see it in color was especially shocking. But despite her repulsion, she was drawn to the craftsmanship of it. The colors, the shading, and the lines were all masterfully drawn. She'd done some painting while in college, and considered her level of talent to fall somewhere between mediocre and pretty good, but her grandfather had been a twisted genius. The pages, though old, were full of vivid energy and alive in their unflinching depiction of death.

Stacia turned the page.

The story followed two twin brothers, both of them butchers. Tony was the successful owner of a meat packing plant. Luciano was a serial killer. Tony knew about Luciano's murderous habits, but because they were family, Tony covered for him. Luciano delivered the remains of his victims to Tony's meat plant to be loaded on the truck with the fat, bones, and entrails; byproducts to be disposed of.

The candle burned down beside her as she read, obsessed with the content, hypnotized by the artwork, revolted in the way that only her family could revolt her.

At the end of the first issue, the brothers' operation took an even more sinister turn when it was revealed where the byproducts and the remains of Luciano's victims were being dumped. In the river lived something otherworldly, something that lay dormant, waiting and needing to be fed, an entity only portrayed as a lumpy black shadow with yellow slits for its eyes. Its hold on Tony's mind was so strong that Tony used Luciano's dark urges to keep the beast satisfied.

The fifth issue ended with the brothers being gunned down by police, and a prophetic message that the creature would rise one day from the bottom of the river and lay siege to the city.

Stacia closed the fifth book, feeling that she now knew something that hadn't been meant for her to know, and couldn't be unknown.

She'd had good reasons for running out on her family, and the story within the pages of the comic served as a less than pleasant reminder. They were filthy rich, emphasis on filthy. She'd heard her grandfather was different, but as distant as he'd been, maybe he hadn't been immune to their inherent ugliness. The contents of the comics had a gritty realism that made her wonder just how much of it had been imagined.

She'd once heard that one of her uncles had stood trial for a series of murders. He'd been acquitted, but people had had their doubts.

And hadn't someone in her family run a meat-packing business back in the 1940s? She was sure of it.

Of the memories that flooded back to her, the most vivid were of waking up in the middle of the night as a little girl and hearing her parents chanting bizarre words that she didn't know and couldn't pronounce.

All of this was so overwhelming because she'd tried so long to forget about it. To live her life as her own person. To let the past stay where it belonged, buried in the dusty catacombs of forgotten history. To put as much distance between her and her family as possible.

But she had stayed in the city and she never regretted that

decision more than now, as she sat digesting the contents of her grandfather's grisly comic book.

Now as the memories came back, she wondered if more would come as the hours ticked by. What was her family really up to? What had her grandfather's role in it been? What was *her* role in it? Her father had always told her she was special.

Stacia started to put the books back in the box, but saw below the other items was a large folder. She debated whether to look inside of it or put the books back and stuff the box far into her closet. For a reason she couldn't explain, she felt a forceful compulsion to pull the folder out and examine its contents. She set the books aside and grabbed it out from under the other items. On the front, in large black letters: "Meat District, The Final, Unpublished Issue."

Her teeth sunk into her lip as she held the folder in front of her. She decided that she had to know where the story went. She thought that except for the notion of the beast's return, everything had been resolved in the fifth issue. The brothers were dead after all.

Sheer curiosity propelled her forward.

From the first page, she could see that the setting was different from before. The full-paged panel showed the city street blanketed in the gray shadows of night. The cars and clothing were modern, more up with today's trends than those of the 1950s. She turned the page, and her breath caught in her throat.

The woman in the next panel had dark hair, worn in a loose bun that hung off the side of her head. She knelt in front of a cardboard box, her face vaguely illuminated by a single candle on the floor.

Stacia was the woman in the picture.

She stared at the artist's rendition. It was impossible, but it was unmistakably her.

The next panel showed her face bathed in white and lightning flashed outside her apartment. Her heart beat furiously in her throat as the roar of thunder almost immediately followed.

A coincidence, she thought, *this has to be*.

She tensed as a foot appeared in frame just behind the image of her in the bottom panel. Spatters of blood clung to the toe of the boot. In the panel after that Tony wore a bloody apron and clutched a meat mallet in his fist. His skin was gray with the sickness of death.

Stacia threw the book down, a yelp bursting from her lips. She frantically glanced behind her, but no one was there.

"Hello?" she called, feeling instantly foolish.

The apartment was silent except for the soft pattering of rain on her balcony window.

She regained control of her breath. With the pages out of her hands, rationale reasserted itself.

It left as quickly as it came when she looked down at the floor and saw a bloody footprint.

She screamed and made her way to the kitchen. Her purse was in there with her cell phone and her mace.

Luciano, the knife-wielding maniac brother, was waiting. His eyes were different than in the comic book. Now enlarged and fish-like they stared at her with predatory intent. His plump lips jutted out in a bloody pucker. More footsteps crept up behind her, sticky with blood and heavy with inevitable doom.

Stacia turned to spring away, but a blunt impact struck the back of her head and knocked her to the floor. White stars exploded in her eyes. Darkness closed in and within the darkness, crimson, blood-spattered entrails fell from the bellies of gutted pigs.

The faces of her family regarded her with newly acquired amphibious features.

The twin butchers carved.

Pages tore and bled.

Dying animals squealed, and dying humans screamed.

Stacia screamed with them.

The darkness had been there all along, in the river and in the blood.

Her blood.

And it swallowed everything.

FOR SALE

BY JONATHAN WOODROW

The Realtor sat alone in his office and stared at the untouched cup of coffee on his desk. On the side of the cup was a picture of himself, right below a caption that read: "Springfield is Bob Hogan Territory". Bob cringed and shook his head. He picked up his file for the Harvey family and shuffled the papers around aimlessly before closing it again and placing it back down on the desk.

There was a call from the front door. He pressed the button. "Yeah."

"It's Harvey."

Bob buzzed him in and stood. Moment of truth. His stomach was tense. His head was tense. Even his feet were tense. And his forehead felt suddenly cold and sweaty. He was searching his jacket pocket for a handkerchief or Kleenex just as Mr. Harvey walked into his office and closed the door.

Much of Bob's interaction with clients was under the pretense of hope. He was selling a dream, or moving someone from their current dream to an even bigger dream. Of course there were times when things weren't working out quite as his clients had hoped, but Bob believed there was a positive spin for just about anything. All he had to do was find it.

But in the case of Mr. Harvey and his family, Bob was stumped for positivity.

Harvey wore scuffed Oxford shoes, rumpled blue shirt and charcoal sport coat, no tie. His hair was ruffled and his eyes were dark and defeated.

"You wanna sit?" Bob asked.

Harvey pulled out a chair.

"Drink?"

Harvey shook his head.

Bob sat down and picked up the file folder again. He resumed shuffling through the papers. "How's Kate?" he asked.

Harvey's expression didn't change. Like something inside him was on hibernation mode. Bob was about to open his mouth to say something else—though what, exactly, he wasn't sure—when Harvey beat him to the punch.

"Save it, please," he said. "I didn't come here for an awkward moment. I just need your help."

Bob nodded and said with measured caution, "Okay, I'm listening."

"My family's been in a hotel now for six weeks. We have all kinds of expenses, debts. And as you know, Kate's been in the hospital ever since... well."

Bob nodded.

"Apparently our home insurance doesn't cover demonic possession."

Bob gave Harvey a wan smile. "And what can I do to help?"

"We're in the red, Bob. Credit cards, lines of credit, all maxed. No nest egg. No family to help out. We need to move this house, now."

Bob hesitated. "You know, with the current—"

"I know. We'll lose money. You said that."

"That's right, but what if you allow the bank to foreclose?"

"Not an option," Harvey said. "I do that, my business goes down the tube and we're in the same boat as we are now."

"Mr. Harvey, just so we're clear. You want me to do, what, exactly?"

"You tell me," he said. And then, "What are we looking at, worst case? I need a ball park number."

Bob exhaled, looked down at the desk. "I'd say, current state of affairs, you'd be looking at a thirty per cent loss. Best you can hope for is you wait a while, maybe find someone from out of town who doesn't do their research."

Harvey shook his head. "Not good enough, Bob. You can do better than that."

Bob opened his mouth but decided to keep quiet. Moving on the defensive wouldn't do any good here. "Tell you what, leave it with me for today, OK?"

● ● ●

Bob had sold the house on Timi Valley to the Harvey family four months earlier. A few days after closing, he'd dropped by a housewarming gift. The gift was a ceramic rendering of a young woman, which bore such a striking resemblance to Kate Harvey that when Kate had noticed it displayed on the mantelpiece during their first viewing of the house, she'd paused midsentence and stared at the statuette for several moments in total silence.

Convinced that the statuette had been a deal maker, Bob had approached the listing realtor after signing to inquire about buying the item from the seller.

Ordinarily, Bob kept a large box full of generic housewarming gifts: mantel clocks, hand-painted vases, faux-antique lamps—all bought in wholesale quantities, of course. But when presented the statuette to Kate Harvey, he knew right away that his small gesture would pay dividends later on. Once again, Kate was entranced, and for three long minutes she caressed the doll, tracing her fingers over its delicate features, running them around the painted pale blue scarf and the long, red hair that cascaded down the statuette's back and flicked playfully up at the bottom; all the while gazing into the dark, haunted eyes that somehow gave the piece a life-force of its own. If he was honest with himself, Bob had found the whole thing a little erotic.

And now, in the wake of all that had followed, this memory exposed raw feelings of guilt that Bob hadn't felt in years.

After some hazy, unfocused consideration, he began his research. For the rest of the evening he worked, digging and delving deep into the dark recesses of society, until he was sure he'd found what he was looking for. A lead. A potential buyer. He picked up the phone and dialed, but the voice that answered did so in a quiet, childlike tone that screamed at Bob's lizard-brain to hang up and run... *run like hell and never look back, just forget about the Harveys, let them deal with their own mess, it isn't worth it... isn't worth...*

"Is this Bob *Logan*?" the pre-pubescent voice squealed in delight. "I was expecting your call." And Bob knew it was too late for any of that now. This was way beyond the last resort, and there would be no turning back.

The next call he made was to Harvey.

• • •

The Blauhardt Towers was a gated community, hiding in plain sight, that placed a heavy emphasis on privacy. To the extent that very few people were even aware of its existence. There was no way the twin low-rise buildings could be considered, in a literal sense, 'towers'. Not by anyone's standards. But Bob understood that the word wasn't used to describe the physical stature of the buildings, but rather its ability to sustain a powerful and gothic, yet invisible presence in a city that otherwise sought to know every little detail about its inhabitants. The complex was veiled by a tall and impenetrable fence, and lined by a thick circle of hundred-year old oaks. It was accessible from only one entry-point, and as Harvey and Bob approached, the twenty-feet tall wrought iron gates rolled open in a smooth, ominous motion and they caught their first full view of the understated concrete cuboids.

They took the elevator up to the fourth floor where they were greeted by the man who called himself Ginger.

"Welcome," he said.

Harvey looked at Bob, who now regretted not prepping him a little on what to expect.

The apartment was indeed large, but the realtor in Bob was struck by how still and lifeless the interior was. Despite the massive bay windows, the light in the main room was dim, somehow drained, and shadows seemed to spill out of the corners and cracks in a way that defied the laws of physics. The unease that Bob was already feeling worsened when he sensed the almost tangible presence of pain and hopelessness, like they were entities in their own right, roaming about the apartment.

What caught his eye was an eclectic presentation of knick-knacks lined up on the dusty mantel piece, and Bob focused on this token of normalcy as an anchor to his sanity. But there was something off about the display. Each piece, he could now see, was damaged in some way. He walked over to the fireplace and leaned in to examine them more closely. On the far right was a stuffed animal with its left arm and part of its leg torn off, the cotton dangling over the edge; next to it was a gold watch with its face covered in thick black paint, and a strap that appeared to be chewed off at the buckle. By contrast, the flaws on some of the other items were barely noticeable, and took a moment for Bob to see. Resting against the wall was an early edition of a short story collection by Algernon Blackwood. At first, it appeared normal, but when Bob looked again, the book was missing thirty or so pages that had been meticulously replaced by slices of deli meat.

Bob heard footsteps and he turned to see a young girl step into the room. The girl held a coffee pot and stared down at the ground as she poured, not once making eye contact.

Harvey said, "So, is someone going to talk about why we're here?"

Ginger looked at Bob and grinned. "Yes, Bob. Why don't we get on with your pitch?"

Bob stood. "I'll make this brief."

"No, please," Ginger said. "Don't spare any details. I love the details."

Bob continued. "Mr. Harvey and his family moved into a house that turned out to have... well... somewhat of an infestation."

"Bob, did I somehow lead you to believe I offered an extermi-nation service?"

Bob smiled, "No, that's not quite—"

Harvey shook his head and stood. "Listen guy," he said. "It's simple."

Bob placed a hand on Harvey's chest, urging him to sit back down, but Harvey pushed him away.

"You want details?" he said. "I can do that. My family and I moved into a dream home that this guy here sold us. Turned out the dream was more of a nightmare. People got hurt. Things became quite public, and now we can't sell the place."

Ginger uncrossed his legs and crossed them again. He ran a hand over his smooth face. "Go on."

Harvey took a deep breath. "It started in Cal's room. Cal's our little one, five years old. Well, he started crying in the night. Something he'd never done before. Not in, what... three or four years? He's always been a great sleeper. And at first we chalked it up to the new house, you know. It would pass, eventually, once he got used to the new place. So we left it. But it didn't stop, and soon he was waking up screaming three, maybe four times a night. I mean really screaming. Running into our bedroom, absolutely terrified, scaring the piss out of me and the wife. So she decided to put a motion activated webcam in there with him, you know, one with night vision, all that. Spent a small fortune. So that's what we did. And when we played back the video."

Harvey paused. Ginger's grin widened and he leaned in. "Mr. Harvey, please, if you will."

"There were shadows, at first. Lots of them. They moved around the room for no logical reason. The shadow from the chair in the corner moved over to the window, inexplicably, and the street light coming in through the blinds slid down onto the ground and over to the bed. And then Cal... all sudden his face started, well, twisting. His mouth would open, wider and wider. Then you'd see his eyes snap open, awake, and he'd scream. The shadows would start swirling around, in a frenzy, and then his arms stretched out, his head fell back, and his face snapped from side to side, like someone was hitting him. Then the bed sheet somehow got itself all wrapped up around his neck like a snake. Choking him. Well, after that, he stayed with us, permanently, and the wife started looking through the Yellow Pages for some kind of ghost hunter. You know, like in that dumb TV show? Well that didn't work out too well, as you'd imagine. This is real life. She made a call to a bunch of places, and people started talking, and then we had kids climbing over our fence, trying to get a look at something... supernatural. I had to scare a few off my property with a shovel." Harvey shook his head, as though steeling himself for the next part of the story. "And then things got a lot worse."

Bob leaned back in his chair and tried to pretend he was somewhere else, but Ginger was completely captivated by Harvey's tale.

Harvey proceeded to tell the story of the house on Timi Valley. He described the game of hide and seek that led Cal out into the busy street. He told them about the time his wife dreamed of being raped by the family dog, and then woke up to find the dog dead on the floor of Cal's bedroom, having apparently chewed off two of its own legs before bleeding out on the rug. And then about how his mother-in-law had suffered multiple lacerations to her oesophagus after eating what she'd thought were cookies but which turned out to be Peter's pet tarantulas. He told of the time Peter, the eleven year old, had climbed up the chimney one night in mid August after becoming convinced that Santa was waiting for him in there with a gift, and how he had gotten himself lodged up there for the better part of a day, barely able to move or breathe, until Harvey found him later on and pulled him down. Peter's face and mouth had been covered in human bite marks and his hair was knotted with brown tinsel. Later that evening, Peter had confessed that he was in love with old Saint Nick, and that this year, instead of the usual letter, he wanted to send Santa a pair of his underwear.

Harvey explained how he would sometimes hear the house laughing at them—a thick, swaying groan that came out in giggles.

But the last story, the one that finally forced them out of the house for good, was the one Ginger was waiting for. As though all that other stuff was foreplay and this was the cum shot.

It was clear to Bob that his client was drained.

"My wife, Kate," Harvey said. " She's currently in a coma."

Bob shut his eyes. This was the part of the story he had experienced firsthand. Ginger's excitement was audible.

"It was the day I first decided to go see Bob about trying to move the house. That was when the house decided to step it up a notch."

Bob stood. "Ah, Ginger, does Mr. Harvey really have to go on. Surely you've heard enough already, no?"

Ginger's smile faltered and he turned and stared at Bob. His eyes were alive with venom. They were the eyes of the predator who's spotted his prey and is hard as a rock with blood and adrenaline, ready to pounce... only to be interrupted at the last minute by a mosquito buzzing in its ear. Bob sat back down again.

To his credit, Harvey seemed unfazed by the pleasure Ginger was taking in his misery.

"Bob and I met in a coffee shop to go over some details. We headed back to the house to talk it over with the wife, and the first thing I noticed was blood on the door handle. Then I saw blood on the tiles in the entry hall, and then there was blood everywhere."

Bob shut his eyes and shook his head.

"As we made our way further into the house, it was all dark, but I could see there were... things, on the floor."

"What things?" Ginger asked, his voice pinched, the two words coming out in staccato.

"Until I turned on the light I wasn't sure. But when I did... I vomited on the floor. The hardwood was drenched in thick, sticky, dark blood. Spread out all over, not a square inch uncovered. And those things I'd seen on the ground, the shapes? They were pieces. Pieces of my kids, scattered about the place like old rubble. And then I heard someone whistling from upstairs, and the red I was seeing seeped into my head and I could see nothing else from that moment but the red, *all the red*. And I kept hearing something like a voice from behind me, calling my name in a distant echo, Harvey, Harvey, hey, Mr. Harvey. But it was way in the background, and the whistling was louder, more present. It drowned everything else out. Then I heard footsteps, and a figure started down the stairs, and it was chewing on something. Something thick and red with hair sprouting out of the top. Red hair. Kate's hair. And the thing said, "Hi, honey, I put dinner on," like an imitation. And so I lunged, driven by the red, and I was on top of the thing, hands around its neck, and I opened my mouth and roared like a lion, and my fists came down and down and down... until I was pulled off by someone... pulled off by Bob here. And all the red evaporated, and lying on the stairs all limp and lifeless was my wife, Kate, sweet Kate, and her face was dark and twisted and my children were screaming from the living room, screaming my name, Daddy, Daddy, Daddy, and tugging at my leg, crying out for their mother, asking me what happened. As if I could tell them..."

Ginger clapped his hands together and whooped like a teenage girl.

Bob felt a deep horror growing inside of him. What had he done?

"And so we left," Harvey continued. "That night, no further procrastination. We told the police a story about how Kate fell down the stairs and the kids didn't know any different so they went along. Bob knew the investigating officer. Had sold him a house or something. Anyway, after Kate was admitted to the hospital and was stable, I took the kids to the Motel 6, checked in, and we haven't been back to the house since."

Ginger snapped his fingers and the little house girl returned and poured another coffee. "Mr. Harvey," he said, his tone was more business now. "You said your wife was stable when you left her at the hospital."

Bob frowned, picking up on the same inconsistency.

Harvey nodded. "Yes, that's right. She was stable."

"But now she's in a coma."

Harvey nodded again. "Yes, that's right."

"So, please go on with your story."

Harvey nodded. "I went to see her the next day, to see what she remembered, if anything at all, and more importantly, to see what she'd been able to tell the nurses, or the police who were hanging around. She was awake when I got there, barely. But she smiled as I walked in. That made me happier than I'd been in months, to see her smile. It meant that things were going to be all right in the end."

"But there was something out of place, wasn't there?" Ginger said.

"Yes. Something on the table by the bed. From the house. I still have no idea how it got there."

"Which was?"

"A statuette."

Bob tensed as he pictured the very gift he'd given to Mrs. Harvey after they'd moved in to the house.

"As I was turning to leave, I heard this awful choking. A tearing, gristly sound coming from the bed." Harvey covered his mouth with his hand and a tear rolled down his cheek and onto his wrist. "As soon as I turned around, lights started flashing and the machines started bleeping and all hell broke loose and Doctors and nurses pushed past me and over to my wife on the bed, shouting and barking orders and getting into position."

"What did you see?" asked Ginger. "Details, details, remember? I need details."

"Kate had swallowed her hand. It was jammed in right up to her elbow. When I saw her, her eyes were rolled back in her head, she was convulsing, her face was purple, blood was trickled out of the corners of her mouth and her throat bulged out all distended. The doctors told me to get out, you know, so they could work. But they knew I had nothing to do with it. By then, they'd all heard about the house. People will tell you they don't believe in that stuff, but a part of them does."

Bob's mouth stayed open for the next few moments, frozen

in shock. This was all too much for him. He wanted to get back to selling houses. Normal houses. To normal families. No excitement, just routine. Surely Harvey knew that Bob had given the statuette to Kate as a gift. He shuddered as a deep sadness seeped into his soul like a stain, and he knew it was there for good.

The room went silent for the next little while, save for the occasional slurping as Ginger finished his coffee. It was Harvey who broke that silence. "So there, I've told my story. What say we move this along."

Bob knew that was his cue, but he no longer had any idea what he was going to say.

Ginger stepped in. "I think Bob here wanted me to make you an offer. For the house. See, I understand it has garnered somewhat of a reputation now, what with the hauntings and all, and as you say, even though most folks tell you they don't believe in that stuff, they're still smart enough to steer clear of it anyway. Just in case they're wrong. So your house is now tainted goods. Am I right?"

Harvey nodded. "That's about the sum of it."

"Good, so what Bob here was thinking was maybe he could find someone who would be interested in not the traditional real estate value of the property, but in the less tangible value of what the house has to offer. Get my meaning?"

"I do."

"And from what I've heard here today, the house has quite a remarkable talent, does it not?"

"I suppose you could say that."

"I most definitely would say that, Mr. Harvey. Now, I'm sure you have to be getting back to the motel, so I'll forego any attempt at a traditional style of negotiation. My offer, first and final, is this: I will pay you one-point-five-million dollars for your house, Mr. Harvey. Not a penny more, not a penny less. That's more than three times what you paid for it. Do we have a deal?"

Bob snapped out of his trance and his mind kicked into Realtor mode—his happy place, finally—but he was too late. Without so much as a flicker of hesitation, Harvey held out a hand

and said, "We have a deal."

Bob looked from Harvey to Ginger, utterly bewildered. "That's it?" he said.

"Almost," said Ginger. "There is one small condition. The statuette. Do you still have it in your possession?"

Bob held up a hand. "Ginger, if you would please allow me to consult with Mr. Harvey before we go any further. I can get back to you with a response later today, but for now—"

"I still have it," said Harvey, cutting him off.

Bob said, "Mr. Harvey, please consider what you're saying. You're a business man. You need time to cool off. Time to think about this with a clear head."

Harvey turned to face his realtor. "What the hell is there to think about, Bob? We all get what we want here, what we need. It's a win-win. Besides, I don't see what you have to complain about here, this gets you... what, seventy grand commission? Commission you don't even need to split. That's all yours. And for what? You made a couple of calls, we took a trip together to see *this* guy, and then you sign some papers. That's... what, four hours work, five, tops? Twelve grand an hour. Why don't you shut the hell up and take the deal, you greedy son of a bitch! You're the reason we're in this mess in the first place." Harvey took a breath, but he wasn't done. "Or, what, let me guess, you're angling for more money? Well no, that's not going to happen, I'm done with this house, and done with all of you. This is our way out, and I will not let you jeopardize that."

Ginger giggled again. It was the giggle of a small child who found humour in watching the starving coyote fall off the edge of a cliff before getting blown up by his own TNT. When he turned his gaze to the young girl who stood in the doorway, her face turned a deathly pale, and Bob was sure he saw her hair rise up from her head like it was trying to stand on end.

Ginger grinned. "I'll have my lawyer send over the paperwork," he said. "Now if you will excuse me, I have other activities on my afternoon schedule."

The deal was done. The contracts signed, the funds trans-ferred. Bob had his lawyer go over the Agreement of Purchase and Sale and he found no irregularities—no catch, no tricky fine print. But this was bad news for Bob. It meant he had no legiti-mate reason to dissuade Harvey from moving forward with the deal. And with that, the Harvey home now belonged to Ginger.

Juggling his work duties, child care responsibilities, and of course the numerous visits to the intensive care unit to check on Kate, Harvey was able to make an unconditional offer on another home on the other side of the city, with a closing period of thirty days.

It seemed the Harvey kids were falling into something resem-bling a routine, which Bob took as a good sign, and best of all, he'd heard Kate's condition was improving.

Bob went to see Harvey on closing to check on things, and he was pleased to find that the new house was perfectly bland and generic; no doubt exactly what Harvey was looking for. The two men shook hands and agreed to part ways amicably. Bob sus-pected this was the last time the two of them would do business, and that was fine by him. There were too many bad memories.

Several weeks went by and Bob was pushing hard for busi-ness. His intention was to flood as much water under the bridge as he could, and he found himself spending every evening and weekend attending viewings and open houses, not to mention all the administrative duties he preferred to handle himself.

One morning, Bob was in the process of knocking a 'For Sale' sign into the front yard of a four-bed exec home in the southern part of town when his cell phone rang. It was his assistant.

"What happened?" he asked, panic rising in his chest for no logical reason.

"I, ah... I just thought you should know, Bob, that Kate Har-vey passed away last night. You remember Kate?"

Bob rolled his eyes. "How?" he asked.

"Apparently some freak accident at the hospital, chemical

burns or something like that. Just awful. Her body couldn't take it. That's all I know."

Bob disconnected the call and got into his car. He drove until he reached the iron gates of the Blauhardt Towers.

Ginger answered the door with a grim look of satisfaction on his face. "What a pleasant surprise," he said.

"Where is it?" Bob asked.

The smile remained perfectly fixed. "Where's what?"

Bob pushed past him and crossed the apartment. In the centre of the mantle, slightly set back and leaning against the wall, was the statuette he'd given to Mrs. Harvey as a gift. Only something was different about it now. He squinted, then gasped. "What happened to it?" he demanded.

Ginger shook his head. "Oh, that. Terrible thing. I was standing right here, admiring the statuette, when all of a sudden it just slipped out of my hands." He held out his hands as though to illustrate. "Damn thing fell straight into the fire. By the time I'd found a suitable utensil to retrieve it I was too late. The surface had been burned, as you can see. It's a real shame, because it was such a beautiful piece, really. And now it's spoiled."

Bob grabbed Ginger by the shirt and lifted him off the ground. Ginger's eyes lit up with delight as Bob carried the small man across the room and slammed him up against the wall.

A low growling brought Bob back to reality.

"My, my, Bob," said Ginger. "You are a passionate man. Strong, too."

Bob lowered Ginger to the ground. When he turned he saw four very large, snarling beasts facing him, teeth bared, a starving look about them. He released his grip and backed away.

Ginger walked over and stood between Bob and the four creatures. "I would invite you to stay for supper," he said. "But I'm sure you have other plans. Lots of houses to be sold. I imagine there's quite a killing to be made, am I right?"

Without another word, Bob walked over to the door and let himself out.

• • •

Bob navigated his way around the city, with no particular destination in mind, and he played the events over and over in his mind, trying to figure out if there was anything he could've done differently, and in a brief moment of almost-clarity, he decided there would be a positive side to all of this. There always was.

And all he had to do was find it.

MAINE COON

BY NICK MEDINA

He slid the window shut just as a wasp flew in; he unaware of the wasp and the wasp unaware that it would never fly out. It was to keep her put that he slid the window shut, forcing her to sit on the sill with her nose against the glass and her eyes and ears tuned to something he had no interest in tending to. He stood back, staring at her for a time, and then she hissed – as he suspected she might – reminding him of that thing she needed him to do.

Quick to dismiss the hiss, he shuffled away from the window only to be reminded once more of the thing she needed him to do, for, laying not two feet from where he stood on the living room floor, was the deflated corpse of a field mouse looking as empty and gray as an abandoned baby bootie.

He gasped at the sight, though he shouldn't have been quite so shocked. Over the past months she'd left several of the same repellent little reminders throughout the house: in the hall, by the door, a particularly grotesque one on the counter in the kitchen and another on the vacant pillow next to the pillow upon which he slept.

This one, though, was the worst of all. Not just killed, lifeless as it was, but ravaged—brutalized in a way that caused its purple insides to protrude from its lower end and which gave an unnatural twist to the neck so that the creature's mouth aimed up, gaping at him. He shuddered, hating that she brought him face-to-face with one of the unwelcome and unsettling scroungers, like the spiders and the roaches, which he tried to rid from his home.

She hissed again, seemingly unaware of his repulsion. She hadn't moved from the window. In fact, she held herself like a stone sphinx, only her green eyes languidly shifting from side to side; this he could tell by the chartreuse reflection skating across the glass. Her composure made him shudder. There she sat responsible for another lost life and yet it bothered her none, as though they were hers for the taking, as though the creatures she killed didn't mind at all.

Inhaling deeply, he reached for the plastic shopping bag he'd abandoned on his chair when she came bounding through the window only minutes before. Using the bag as a glove, he bent and pinched the tail of the repellent dead thing while pinching his nose with his naked right hand. Sorry as he might have felt for the loss of life, he couldn't regret that the mouse was dead. It and others like it had invaded his home throughout the previous winter, gnawing holes in his walls and chewing through his cracker boxes, cookie bags and even a small corner of the bread bin too, leaving small, black droppings mixed with the crumbs they selfishly left behind. It was only then, as he was carrying the drippy mess away from the living room floor that she turned away from the window. Hopping from the sill upon which she was perched, she trailed him into the kitchen, even weaving through his legs at one point, to see what he'd do with the mutilated vermin she'd gifted him.

He went straight through the kitchen to the backdoor that opened up onto a walkway overlooking the alley. Without stopping to consult her, without even turning to glance at her sitting so perfectly proper and composed on the yellow linoleum, he whipped the door open and tossed the dead thing out. A second or so later a thud echoed up from below, reinforcing the reality of the mouse's misfortune.

He closed the door quickly and put the lock in its place as

though the horror he'd just disposed of would sneak back in if he left the apartment unsecured for more than a second or two.

Relief welling within him, he spun away from the door only to have his face fall when he caught her staring up at him, questioning him, perhaps. They both held stock-still, just glaring, each communicating a misinterpreted message.

Her green eyes cut into him, and though he knew she was sharp, he couldn't help but melt for her, his only companion. He stepped closer, stooping to scratch behind her ear, but she skulked away, leaving his fingertips reaching for nothing but empty air.

He didn't see her throughout the afternoon that followed, though he had no doubt that she was there because she had no way of getting out of the apartment. She'd have hidden beneath his chair or behind the radiator. Once he found her wedged between the lowest shelves of the roll top desk he never sat behind, but which he used to hold his countless receipts and the crinkled, crumpled plastic bags he saved.

He thought she'd come running when she heard him drop a handful of food in her dish, but that didn't bring her forth any more effectively than the rapid *tss, tss, tss* he made with his tongue. Really there was only one thing that would get her out from where she had hidden, and that was the window.

* * *

It was dark when he saw her again, and he only saw her for a split second through the corner of his eye when he finally relented and raised the windowpane. The blur of her heavily-furred tail, chocolate in color and thick as a rolled up rug, competed with the darkness beyond the open window, and then she was gone, her frenzied footsteps rattling the fire escape, linked by fixed iron balconies, down to the bottom floor from where she jumped to the street.

She worried him in moments like that, and instantly he knew that he shouldn't have raised the window, though she'd have grown angry if he hadn't. But still, he knew she'd grow angry out there on her own as well. She had a life in the streets that precluded him. A life full of events of which he was unaware, but though he knew little of what she did while she was away, he knew that her nights were ruined by vermin of her own, because, when she did inevitably return, she'd sit by the window and hiss.

A sudden series of knocks rattled him away from his worry. Beckoned to the front door, he shuffled through a mess of plastic and paper bags he'd piled along the floor, to press his bespectacled eye against the peephole for a glance into the hall.

A face as wrinkled as if it had been a piece of paper crumpled into a tight ball and then stretched out again to only half its original size filled the glass.

"Miss Cohen," he muttered, pressing his glasses lens flush against the peephole once more just to make sure he'd really seen his landlady and not some other withered face.

"Open the door, Edgar," she said, putting his nerves at ease just a tad bit more by proving that she knew his name.

Slowly he undid the lock, leaving the chain in place. The old woman opened the door for him, pushing it in until it met the resistance of the chain, the harsh jolt of which made her cry out.

"Oh, Edgar," she said, "you and that damn chain." He didn't say anything in response. He merely tottered back and forth by the door, his anxious eyes taking in the minutest details of his un-manicured fingernails.

"It's your rent," she said, sounding like his mother as she waved the check he'd slipped beneath her door in the five-inch gap afforded by the chain. "It's four-fifty, not four-hundred. I've told you six times since January. I had to raise the rent."

"Four-fifty," he echoed, somewhat questioning, still examining his fingernails.

"Four-fifty. Just like last month and the month before, though you're lucky I haven't raised it more for bringing in that damn cat." Her saggy face fell even more when she frowned. Communicating with him was harder than trying to fall up the stairs rather than down.

He nodded and retreated from the door, shuffling through the bags once more.

"Didn't I tell you about this mess?" she called after him, waving a rickety finger in the space of the door instead of his rent check this time. "Those bags are ripe for fire. Get rid of them before they spark a blaze. Lord knows you'll burn me up."

"They're plastic," he muttered, escaping her line of sight as he located the old cigar box with his money inside, "not wood." "Everything burns. Remember that, Edgar," she said, tightening her knotty fingers like roots around his wrist when he went to hand her the money he owed. "Clean up this mess. It's no wonder we have rats." She dropped his wrist as she retreated to the apartment beneath his.

"But they can hold things," he said of the bags, simultaneously pondering whether the mice that ate his food were really rats and if he indeed was the one responsible for their presence. He couldn't be, he decided. Besides, they'd stopped stealing from his cabinets right around the time he got the cat. Now it was she who brought them into the apartment.

Knowing that it would be fruitless, but hopeful nonetheless, he went to the window and leaned his head outside. Calling for her with clicks of his tongue and rapid taps against the windowsill, he scanned the fixed-escape balconies and the street below for any hint of her. She wasn't in sight, of course. She wouldn't be back until morning. And then she'd remind him once again of that thing she needed him to do.

• • •

He bent to see what it was, his eyes pinched, his nose no more than a foot away from it on the floor. It was black and small, furry like a kiwi, but clearly not. It didn't dawn on him at first that it had come from her, though he was aware of her sitting above him, perched amid the many volumes on the highest shelf of the bookcase, her tail twisting from left to right like curling smoke. He leaned another inch closer and then gasped.

His repulsion sent him so far backward that he banged his hip against the desk, causing him to limp forward again whereupon he grasped the back of the couch for support.

She didn't move a single inch in that instance. Her eyes stayed fixed on him, her tail still languidly swaying from side to side.

"Bat," he wheezed. That's what it was on the floor – part of a bat, anyway. The little black ball was just a torso; the leathery wings were gone, ripped away.

Thoroughly disgusted, he locked eyes with her because he knew she'd brought the night flyer in. Moreover, he knew that she had terrorized it. Silently asking why with his eyes, he got his answer soon enough, remembering that it was he who had voiced his dislike of the mysterious creatures he sometimes heard flittering about when he opened the window for her at night. Mice with wings, he'd called them. She must have heard. And understood.

A shiver went down his spine just as a gust of wind blew in through the window. He looked at her again and then propelled himself across the room intent on shutting the window for good this time, but she leapt from the bookcase when he did and landed on the sill ahead of him. Emitting a quick hiss, she was gone, and he couldn't help but notice who she had hissed at. It was, as always, Miss Cohen on the balcony below, tending to her flower boxes the way she did every morning. The old woman swatted at the cat with a hand shovel, actually throwing the mouser off balance on her way down to the street, which was much worse than the rolled-up newspaper Miss Cohen usually used. On the verge of crying out, he pulled his head back inside the apartment just in time to avoid the woman's upturned accusatory scowl.

Slightly dizzy, his hip still throbbing, he gripped the sash, wondering if he should slam it shut.

He didn't see her for two days after that, though she let her presence be known. He found, it seemed, one of her little reminders at every turn: not just mice, but an occasional bat and even insects he'd never encountered before. There were so many that he'd bag one only to find another had taken its place, ultimately causing him to lose track of the one he'd just bagged until it turned up again when he reached for an apparently empty sack, which, unfortunately and inevitably, he'd put his hand within without looking only to find a battered corpse at his fingertips.

The feel of them, moist and soft, sometimes warm as their life had only just left them, bred panic within him, which came pouring out over his lips. The screams earned the attention of Miss Cohen downstairs, but, sensing no imminent danger behind them, perhaps because he'd had outbursts before, she never did anything more in response than bang against her ceiling with the broom she kept by the door.

Danger or not, the anxiety escalated within him as his home became a boneyard for all the things that gave him dread, things he'd only ever wanted gone. And before he knew it he was flat in bed, barely able to breathe, his blanket and sheet pulled tight up around his head, too ill and overcome to even give thought to closing the window.

It was then as he was bundled in bed that he heard her return. The soft stomps of her padded paws made a ring around the room, coming to a stop at the foot of the bed whereupon a final thump sounded, suggesting it was more than just her rump hitting the floor.

Unable to move, and even more reluctant to look for fear of what he might find, he clenched his eyes shut and dulled his hearing by moaning so loud that he became the only thing that he could hear. Inevitably the obstructions, along with his escalating unease, allowed the walls of his mind to grow tall and tight, creating a fortress constructed without a door. Imprisoned in his head, it wasn't his utter abhorrence of the damned things she delivered that paralyzed him; it was his acute knowledge of what he'd have to do to make it all stop – to make her stop – that rendered him so immobile that all he could do was wail.

Eventually the merciful grasp of a dreamless sleep, closely akin to death, freed him from his horror, but when he did reawaken – some hours later, his senses fully restored – his first thought wasn't of her or what she might have dropped; it was of the window. Somehow he had to get it closed, and whether she was in or out hardly seemed to matter, though deep down he didn't want to lose her no matter what her demands.

Still encumbered by the blanket and sheet wrapped around his head, he stripped them away to find that the pressure on his chest, of which he'd only been vaguely aware since waking, was actually her resting upon him.

He startled at the initial sight of her, but then relaxed as relief washed over him, just happy to have her back. His muscles loosening, he fell deeper into the mattress and reached to scratch her behind the ears. When he did, however, he couldn't help but notice the ugly crust clinging to the lion-like ruff of fur around her neck.

"Blood," he gasped, his fingers falling away. It wasn't just in her mane, it was dried to her whiskers, on her paws and even along the furry tips of her ears.

Sickened, he pushed her away and sprang from the bed; a regrettable move since his left foot landed on something frail yet substantial, something that grossly deflated beneath his weight.

"No," he screamed, repeating the word over and over again. At every turn as he reeled he found another and another. All the things that he hated. All dead.

Falling to his knees, he buried his head against the mattress upon which she still sat. Beneath his sobs he could hear her purring. When he lifted his head to look at her, she wrapped herself around his face in a reassuring caress, drying his tears with her fur as though to tell him everything would be all right.

Slightly more stable than before, his mind turned toward the window once again, the thought of which brought him to his feet and out to the living room. There were more corpses in the hall along the way, and when he got within sight of the window, he had to stop because of what he found.

Bile rose in his throat at the sight while his stomach churned, turning his bowels to liquid. Overcome by shock, he staggered backward, unaware that she'd silently followed him out of the bedroom. Feeling her at his feet, however, he had to throw himself forward, closer to the horror, to keep from kicking her.

Inches shy of the window, he stood in disbelief of what was splayed before him. A pigeon, split straight down the middle, stared up at him with an unending gaze.

Of all the things he hated, he hated pigeons most. This, too, she knew, because he had made a big deal about shooing them off the balcony. He'd even tied a stuffed hawk to the rails to scare them off, but that only worked for a while and now he was back to brushing them away with a broom.

Juddering from the inside out, he cautiously approached the bird as though in death it could peck, scratch and infect him more than when it was alive.

She jumped up onto the sill next to her victim, propelling his hand to reach for the window so that she couldn't kill again, but she made no attempt to leave this time. Her attention was on him now, and she was purring again. In the minutes that followed, with him wavering between tears of joy and tears of fright, she looked out the window only once and that was to hiss at the old woman on the balcony below.

Her final reminder hit him hard, effectively reducing him to tears that were neither of joy nor of fright, but something else altogether. She'd done for him, though he'd never asked her to do the things she did, and now he'd have to do for her.

"I understand," he said, retreating from the window. She went on purring as he backed toward the door, where he undid the lock and freed the chain. With one last look over his shoulder at her, he found her licking away the blood, almost as though she enjoyed the taste. And with that, he was gone, his footsteps plodding down the stairs to the apartment below. It wasn't long after that that the woman was gone from the balcony, but it was a long while before he and Miss Cohen were seen again.

When he did return, he burst through the door, chest heaving, sweat coursing down his brow, speckles of red decorating his hands, chest and neck.

He locked the door quickly and barreled into the living room where she was still sitting by the window, clean now, her coat as glossy as the cover of a magazine.

"There!" he declared, heaving the burden draped over his shoulder onto the floor. The bulge, wrapped in a sheet, hit down hard. She glared at it for a while, her eyes pinched tight, but showed no more interest than that.

His mind raced in response. He'd done what she'd wanted him to do. It'd been months in the making, but now her greatest annoyance was gone.

"Here," he said, kicking away the sheet so that she'd be able to see what he'd brought her.

She looked again, still showing very little of the appreciation he expected, and then turned away from his presentation entirely, choosing the window over him once more.

A moment of uncertain silence went by and then, to his dismay, she hissed. Wanting to dismiss what he heard, he reeled to the opposite end of the room only to have her hiss longer and louder than before.

"What?" he cried. Launching himself at her, he stopped just short of doing her harm. Though he hated to look, he followed her gaze to the storefront across the street and found in her line of sight a man he'd only ever seen from the window before.

She hissed.

"More?" he cried. And then it dawned on him that her vermin, like his, went beyond just one. She, in her own way, had done her part to ensure that his would bother him no more, and now he was obliged to do the same for her.

Trembling again, he sat at the desk to plot this time. Surprising as it seemed, a plan came quickly, and before the day was done there were two horrendous bundles on the living room floor.

Certain of her satisfaction now, he sat in his chair with her on his lap. She gently purred while he stroked her back. All was right, it seemed. But when he dozed and woke to the sound that should have existed only in his dreams, his first reaction was to scream.

She was at the window again, looking down at something he couldn't see. Hesitant to join her, the sand of sleep in his eyes, he overcame the hurdles to stand beside her at the window. Believing it to be the darkness, he scanned the street intently, but even after flicking the sand from his eyes, he still couldn't see anyone there. Her hisses were coming faster now, confusing him all the more, and when he turned his eyes upon her he saw that her hisses had nothing to do with the window at all. She'd leapt to the couch and was still making her noises there.

"No," he said, giving his eyes to the street in a desperate search to find someone there. But the block was empty. The street was still. And as such, his transgressions were for naught.

Unable to breathe, he lumbered toward her, the ruthless killer that she was, a misinterpreted murderer, it seemed, who wanted nothing in return other than an occasional scratch behind the ears.

He wasn't going to hurt her. He still couldn't do that. Not even when he dropped down beside her and she hissed at him.

ANATOMY OF A RAPE

BY SANDRA SEAMANS

Everyone's life is driven by the unexpected events and atrocities that rise up to beat the shit out of them. No one is exempt. It's just life. Look at me. I was a law-abiding citizen, a single mom raising a son, just a regular person trying to live a normal life. But under all that normal I knew just how fast an act of violence could tear a person's life apart.

For the past thirteen years I've been clinging to normal, using the crush of ordinary to push back the terror that lives inside my house, pretending that it doesn't exist. But it's always there. Gnawing away at me. Waiting to pounce.

How could I have known that anything as innocent as my son's backpack would change the course of my life? And his.

Caleb's camouflaged-colored backpack was leaning against the porch railing when I headed out for work that morning. I figured he'd set it down on the porch, then forgot to grab it when the school bus stopped for him. Caleb had developed the exasperating habit of drifting off into a world of daydreams that appealed to him more than real life. This lapse into his own private world often resulted in lost shoes, forgotten homework, and now, a misplaced backpack. It was the inexplicable bursts of anger following these lapses that troubled me the most. I tried to convince myself that the change was the result of hormones, the merging of a boy into manhood, but I knew deep down that wasn't true.

With a sigh I tossed the bag in the car, planning to drop it off at the school on my way to work, but my cell phone rang and the past dropped back in my lap for another dance.

"Hello?"

"Mizzz Drake?"

I could feel the cold sweat beading up on my back. I shivered. My hands gripped the steering wheel tighter. I knew that voice. Under his words I could hear the sound of his zipper sliding down, feel the knife at my throat and the hard ground beneath me as... I tried to shake the memory off. I didn't want to go back there. Back to the night when this nightmare began. I didn't want to hear what he had to say but I had no choice. Not then. Not now. He'd come for his son, just like he said he would.

I took a deep breath and said, "Yes."

"I have Caleb."

I pulled the car off to the side of the road. "I thought as much when I heard your voice. You've got what you want, we're done now, right?"

"Done? We're just getting started. Now it's time to play stay alive. There's a bomb in the boy's backpack. Do what you're told and you might make it through the day. Call the cops and you're dead. If you don't follow my instructions, you're dead. Do you understand?"

My hands were shaking and I could barely think. Hadn't he done enough damage to my life all ready? What more did he want from me? Why couldn't he just take the boy and leave?

"Do you understand, Mizzz Drake? It's a simple question, answer yes or no."

"Yes." What choice did I have but to play along with his perverted game?

"Good. Now throw your phone outside the car. You'll find another one in your glove compartment. That's the one we'll be using from now on, so be sure you don't lose it."

I glanced in the rearview mirror and spotted a red pickup pulled off the road behind me. I closed my phone and dropped it out the window. As soon as it hit the ground the new phone started ringing. What he asked me to do made no sense. I knew he had no intention of letting me live, but if there was even the smidgeon of a chance that I could spin this madness back on him, I wouldn't hesitate to do what he asked.

Following his instructions, I walked into First National as the bank opened for business. I showed the teller the bomb with all its blinking lights and colored wires. She emptied her drawer, quickly sliding the money across the counter towards me. I stuffed the money into the empty portion of the backpack, hoping the bomb wouldn't go off as I zipped it closed.

Hurrying towards the door I heard her scream, "That woman has a bomb."

I ran. I had the vague impression of customers either dropping to the floor or standing about with their mouths hanging open. Only the security guard seemed to have his wits about him. As he moved in to tackle me, he was brought up short by a bullet smashing through the front window. I caught a blur of red pulling away from the curb as the guard's body spun sideways before dropping to the floor. I kept going, my frazzled mind racing faster than as my feet. What kind of mad game was he playing at?

Outside, the phone rang again. "Yeah," I said. My feet were chewing up sidewalk, as I ran for my car.

"Forget your car. Turn right at the intersection and walk two more blocks to Sid's Parking Garage. There's a black SUV near the exit on level two. The keys are above the visor and the GPS has been uploaded with your destination."

"Why did you shoot the guard?" I asked, but I was talking to dead air.

A black Dodge Durango was parked two spaces down from the level two exit. I opened the back door and placed the bomb inside, but hesitated before getting behind the wheel. The man had kept me running at top speed since I answered his call this morning. I tossed the phone on the front seat and stepped away from the car, hoping for a few minutes to clear my head. I heard the phone ring and an explosion rocked the garage.

The blast slammed me down onto the concrete floor, embedding a piece of shrapnel from the Durango into my arm. Burning bits of the bank money were floating through the air like a fiery green snowstorm. There was blood oozing from a cut above my eye, but I could finally see clearly. Making me rob the bank wasn't about the money, it was about making me the bad guy. The security guard was shot because he tried to stop me. The bastard couldn't take the risk that I might tell the cops about Caleb. And he was living with the hope that the cops would be so relieved that I was dead they wouldn't bother to investigate past the body bag.

But he hadn't figured on me not being in the car. There would be no body bag. He would know I was still alive and he'd come back for me. I needed to get out here and find a place to hide where he couldn't find me.

I pulled the piece of metal from my arm and wrapped my scarf around the wound to slow the bleeding. I tore off a strip of my blouse to wipe the blood from my face then headed for the exit. The sound of sirens was drawing closer and I knew it wouldn't be long before the streets were filled with fire trucks, ambulances, and cops.

I moved quickly, but not so fast that I'd draw attention to myself. I couldn't afford to have some cop recognize me as the woman who'd just robbed First National and shot a security guard. His plan was perfectly designed. Even if I survived the bomb blast, I couldn't go to the police. They'd never believe such a far-fetched story. Playing dead was my only advantage. My only chance of escape.

At the exit, I scanned the street looking for the red pickup. I didn't see it anywhere. Was he that confident that his bomb would dispose of me? I couldn't take a chance. I ducked my head, and moved in with a group of people who were nearly trampling each other to get outside. I managed to wiggle out of the crowd and slip into an alley before anyone noticed the blood on my clothes.

There was the usual knot of homeless people squatting in the alley, their big cardboard boxes leaning at drunken angles, much like their owners. I found a vacant space near a dumpster and sat down, hoping to blend in with the invisible mass of humanity that made the alley their home. The rancid smell of garbage, puke, and urine stalked the air as shock set in and my body began to shake uncontrollably.

A brown paper sack with the lip of a bottle sticking out was shoved under my nose and a raggedy man said, "Looks like you could use a jolt."

I stared up at his face, saw the edge of kindness under the dirt and grime, and took the bottle. The cheap whiskey burned down my throat, but I stopped shaking. I coughed and choked for a minute then handed the bottle back.

"My name's Amos," said the man as he slid down next to me. "You don't look like you belong here."

"It's been a rough morning and the day's not looking to get any better."

"Maybe I could help? Seems to me you need to get your feet back where they belong, not be crashing here in this alley."

"Crashing. Yes, that's exactly what's happening. A man kidnapped my son this morning and now he's trying to kill me."

"The boy's daddy?"

I stared at Amos, wondering how he knew.

He saw the question in my face and shrugged, "The hardest thing in life is trying to protect the ones you love, most especially if they don't want protecting."

"The boy doesn't even know his father."

"That don't make no difference. Most kids want what they don't have. And boys, they want their daddies. Makes no difference to them how good or bad a man he is. They want that father son connection."

"The truth is, I'm not even sure I want my son back. His father is an evil man. He raped me, forced me to carry his child. And now, when I finally have a chance to pull my life back together he turns it into another nightmare. I can't even go to the cops and explain myself."

Amos tipped his head to stare at me. "That explosion? It was meant for you, wasn't it?"

I nodded my head. "With me dead, no one will challenge his claim to the boy. I have no family, there's nobody to miss him when he's gone except me."

"You must've known this was coming. Somehow, some way, you knew and you've got an escape plan in place, don't you?"

I took a deep breath and let out a long sigh. "Of course, the bomb pushed everything out of my mind. There's a man, he's been helping me get ready for this day. I just need to get to his place before the cops figure out I wasn't in the car when it exploded."

"Boyfriend?" asked Amos.

"No, an old war buddy of my father's, Jake Slocum. They were in Viet Nam together. Jake came home, my father didn't. He's been looking out for me ever since. Jake owns the Army Surplus store over on Kenyon. He'll help me figure this out."

People in the alley were starting to shuffle around, some hiding deeper in their boxes, others moving out of the alley. Amos stood and stretched his hand out. I hesitated a moment then took his hand, allowing him to pull me to my feet. A pair of police officers were coming down the alley. Amos slipped the bottle into his pocket for safekeeping, then grabbed an old blanket from the shopping cart beside him and wrapped it around my shoulders.

He handed me a battered baseball cap then said, "C'mon. They're maybe looking for one of you, not two of us. Keep your fancy duds covered up so you don't look like some do-gooder on the prowl. You don't want them asking questions you can't answer."

I pulled the hat brim down low over my eyes and followed along as he pushed the cart away from the cops. I don't know why, but I trusted him. Maybe that sounds foolish, trusting a complete stranger, but I needed a friend or at least a friendly shoulder to lean on. Someone who gave a damn whether I lived or died.

"Hey you, with the cart," came a voice behind us.

Amos grabbed my arm to keep me from running. "Yes, sir," he said, turning to face the two officers.

The one pointed his baton at me. "There's blood on her hand. Were you near the explosion in the parking garage? Did you see anything?"

I looked at the blood dripping off my hand then shook my head no.

"Then how come you're bleeding?"

"She come up on the wrong side of a knife, officer. That's all," said Amos, swinging his paper bag in the air. "Ain't nothing a little Johnny Walker can't cure."

A giggle bubbled up out of my throat and raced full scale into hysterical laughter. The cops backed off.

"Pair of drunks," said the officer as they turned to leave the alley. "Wouldn't know a bomb if it blew them to Kingdom Come."

Amos grabbed my shoulders and shook me, but I couldn't stop laughing. Tears were running down my cheeks and I was doubled over trying to catch my breath when Amos slapped me. Not once, but twice. I caught his hand on the third swing.

"Enough," I said. "Thanks for the help, but I'll go on by myself from here."

I watched as his eyes drifted toward the madness that had landed him on the streets. He took a long swig from his bottle and said, "Violence breeds violence. Watch your back, baby girl. Now give us a hallelujah and pass the green beans."

And with those strange and ominous words the kind man who had helped me slipped back into his own tortured past.

• • •

Avoiding police patrols and concerned citizens slowed me considerably but I finally worked my way over to Kenyon Street and Jake's store. My arm was throbbing right along with my head and I wanted nothing more than to lay down and forget this morning ever happened. But that wasn't an option. Not today. Today I had to put miles between myself and the mess Caleb's father had created for me. Tomorrow I could sleep.

The lights were on in the store but the closed sign was still hanging in the window and the doors were locked. That wasn't like Jake. He always opened promptly at eight. I slipped around back of the store and climbed the stairs to Jake's upstairs apartment. The key was on the doorsill and I let myself in.

"Jake," I yelled. "Jake, are you in here?"

My voice echoed through the silence. Where was Jake? I used the inside staircase to go down to the store. I found Jake on the floor behind the counter. I pressed my fingers to his neck, praying, but he was dead.

On the floor beside him was a backpack. Caleb's? I unzipped it slowly. Inside were my son's school books and the lunch I'd packed for him. But why kill Jake? How could that bastard know about Jake? It didn't make any sense. Besides, Jake wouldn't let anyone get close enough to slit his throat like that. Unless he used Caleb for a shield.

There was a knock on the door and I crouched lower hoping whoever was out there would go away. I couldn't be seen here. I duck-walked back toward the stairs. After a quick glace to see if Jake's customer had finally given up, I flipped off the lights, and headed back upstairs.

I wanted nothing more than to run. To run as far and as fast as I could to get away from Jake's dead body, from the horror that I was drowning in. But I couldn't. Everything I needed to escape was here. Jake and I had spent the last year preparing for this day and still we were taken by surprise. Well, if I was going down, I was going down fighting. Jake deserved that much from me.

I went into the bathroom, stripped off my clothes and stepped into the shower to scrub the blood off my body. After the shower I tended to the gash above my eye, pulling it together with a couple of butterfly Band-aids. The cut on my arm was deeper and needed stitches. There was a needle and suture thread in the first aid kit, gritting my teeth I started sewing. Thirteen stitches, then a bandage.

In Jake's bedroom I reached under his bed and pulled out a leather duffle bag. Inside were fresh clothes, a new identity, and enough money to get me far away from here. I'd tried running once before, but he found me. Waking up in a strange hotel room with his knife tight against my neck convinced to come back home. Maybe if I hadn't taken Caleb with me he would have let me disappear. I don't know. I lifted the gun Jake had tucked inside and checked to make sure it was loaded, then returned it to the duffle.

I set Jake's Mr. Coffee up to brew and flipped on the TV. My face was plastered all over the news, the picture taken from the bank's security tapes. They were still trying to decide if I'd been killed by my own bomb or not. I was sorta safe. If people thought I was dead they wouldn't be searching faces looking for me. I filled a thermos with the coffee, packed a few sandwiches, and left Jake's apartment, pausing only to grab his cell phone.

Out in the parking lot, I climbed into an old Ford pickup that I'd purchased with my new identity. It was the sort of vehicle no one would expect me to own. Once I was outside of the city, I used Jake's phone to call the police, then tossed the phone. I couldn't bear the thought of Jake not being found. He deserved better from me, but I knew he'd understand.

I drove, on and on for what seemed like forever. I drove until I caught myself falling asleep at the wheel, the blaring of a air horn pulling me back from a near collision with a tractor trailer. I decided it was time to find a motel and get some sleep. There was no point killing myself to make his life easier.

But sleep didn't come, as soon as my head hit the pillow my brain kicked into overdive playing back the day's memory feed. Did I really hear my son giggling in the background when he told me to rob the bank? Was that really Caleb's smiling face in the red truck as it sped away from the bank? Could the sweet boy I raised really be a part of his father's madness? Could I have raised a child who delighted in seeing a person suffer? My body shook at the thought of the horror I might have unleashed into the world.

My downward spiral was interrupted by the sound of tires crunching gravel and headlights penetrating the cracks in the window curtains. I rolled off the bed and crawled across the floor to my duffle bag searching inside until my hand curled around the gun butt. Shaking I worked my way over to the window. Could he have found me already? Was I never going to be safe?

I edged back the curtain to see a couple making their way across the parking lot. They were all over each other, their fingers working furiously to undo hooks, buttons, and zippers. I half expected them to start screwing right there in the parking lot, but they managed to make it inside their motel room. I watched the parking lot for a red pickup until I started to nod off. I pulled a pillow and a blanket from the bed and stretched out in front of the door, my gun tucked under the pillow. I wasn't going to let him take me by surprise again.

The sound of giggling voices woke me. The sun was just coming up and I saw the woman from last night picking her bra up off the ground and looping it around her companion's neck. She pulled him closer and melted into his arms. I envied them their freedom. Oh how I wanted to feel that free.

After they left, I flipped on the TV. My face, again, all over the screen. I was a one woman crime spree wanted for bank robbery, terrorism, and the murder of both the security guard and my friend Jake Slocum. My rapist had done a splendid job of making it impossible for me to... to do what? My son was gone and with that came a sense of loss but also a great relief. That man would be gone from my life forever. I would be able to live without fear, to finally have a bit of peace in my life. But he couldn't let me have that. He was all about the rape and he'd just raped me again.

I wanted to cry or scream or just kill myself. Instead, I tossed the pillow and blanket back on the bed and went to take a shower. I scrubbed and scrubbed until my skin felt raw and still I could feel him next to me. No amount of water was ever going to wash away what he'd done, what he was still doing to me.

Now, every person reaches a point in their life where they either stand up and fight or just lay down and die. I'd been nothing more than a puppet for this man's entertainment for the better part of thirteen years. He pulled the strings and I jumped, my fear of dying stealing away my very soul. Amos was right. The heart wants what the heart wants and I wanted my freedom back. All I had to do was follow the puppet master's strings back to him. A man doesn't invade your life without leaving something of himself behind. I just need to find the bread crumb trail.

● ● ●

Once more I was back on the road, traveling no where in particular. Well, that wasn't exactly true. My memories were pushing me forward. Towards what, I didn't know and the truth was I didn't care. My life was a mess and only by going backwards could I find a way out.

For thirteen years I'd pushed all the memories as far back in my mind as I could, trying to forget what happened that night and all the nights since. Much as I hated the idea, I forced myself to go back through the past, back to that night in the park when I first felt the blade of his knife on my throat. I kept reminding myself that the memories couldn't hurt me but he could.

So I let my mind wander until I could feel the scratch of his beard on my cheek, the smell of beer and onions on his breath as he whispered in my ear, "You're not going to do anything that will kill the boy I just planted in your belly. No hospital. No morning after pill. You do and I'll be back to fuck you again and again until he's growing big inside you. Do you understand me, woman?"

I nodded as a trickle of blood made its way down my neck.

"You'd best remember what I said, 'cause I'll be watching."

Next came the bomb threat that emptied the abortion clinic the day of my apointment. He left a bloody knife in my bed that night. He didn't need any words to tell me that he was watching.

At that moment I knew, without a doubt, there was no escape.

His child grew inside my belly, squirming like a nest of snakes waiting the chance to strike. I was sure he'd be there to scoop up his son the day I delivered. I wanted to be rid of this child, not just from my body but from my life. I wanted both of them gone. Instead a dozen blood red roses arrived. Printed on the card was a simple message. His name is Caleb Everett.

And then the years of torture. His voice on the baby monitor. Christmas presents under the tree. Birthday presents on the kitchen table. The occasional knife in my bed when I did something he didn't like. Last summer was the forced vacation. A week's stay in a cottage on Loomis Lake where Caleb could use the fishing pole his father had left on his twelfth birthday.

With the remembrance of the lake the pieces started to fall together. The little country store where the owner asked if we were related to the Everetts. No? Well, it's danged amazing how much my son looks like the Everett family that lives up the road apiece. Now I knew who he was and where he lived. I headed for the lake. One way or another, everything was going to change.

* * *

Four hours later the truck was bumping over the rutted driveway that lead to the Everett farm. The house was made of weathered boards that hadn't seen paint since the day it was slapped together. It listed to the east and looked like a good strong wind would turn it into a pile of rubble. There was no sign of the red pickup.

I parked the truck near the house. There was no point in hiding, I been doing that for far too long. It was time to stiffen my spine and take back my life. Sounds brave now, but I was scared to death. I tucked the gun into my coat pocket, opened the door, and stepped out. I was reaching for the shotgun on the cab's gun rack when a voice stopped me.

"You'd best leave that gun right where it's at."

Turning I found myself facing the twin barrels of a shotgun

that looked bigger than the woman holding it.

"You must be Caleb's mother. My boy said you was a smart one. You might as well come on in. The boys ain't here right now but they'll be back directly."

I climbed the flagstone steps to the porch and followed the woman inside. She pointed at the table and told me to sit down. Leaning the shotgun against the plank wall beside the door, she turned to the cupboard and took down two coffee mugs, filled them with hot water and tossed a tea bag in each.

"You want milk or sugar?" she asked.

"I don't want your tea. I've come to end this."

"Well, you've come on a fool's errand. What I'd like to know is how you found us."

"It wasn't hard. First I got a note telling me to name the boy Caleb Everett. Then your boy informs me we're taking a vacation up here in the mountains where everyone I meet tells me how much my son resembles the Everett family. It was a simple matter of getting directions for my long-lost kin."

"That boy never did have much for smarts. That's why I sent him down to find you. I wanted a woman with more than a pretty face and a good figure to mother my grandson."

"You sent your son to rape me?"

"Course, you wouldn't have had him no other way. Not your kind."

"What kind of a woman are you?"

"The kind who takes care of her family. Being raped didn't hurt you none, did it? Taking a woman by force makes the baby a fighter. We Everetts been breeding that way for generations."

My hands clenched tightly around the mug of tea. I wanted to throw it in her face, instead I lifted it to my lips, taking a swallow that scalded all the way down my throat. Didn't hurt me? I can still feel my flesh tearing, feel the burn of the hot water on my skin as I tried to shower away all trace of him. I rubbed my skin raw and doused myself with perfume trying to eradicate his smell. But the scent of beer and onions tinged with cigarette smoke remained forever, as did the thin scar on my neck where his knife bit into my skin.

"Didn't hurt me?" I said. "He turned my life inside out. Made me live in fear of a repeat performance. You have no idea of the damage he's done. My son doesn't belong with the likes of you."

"His son. Not yours."

"There is nothing of your son in Caleb. He's a gentle boy. Not a monster, like your son."

"Don't kid yourself. That boy is all Everett, from his looks to his attitude. He's a smart one, that boy. Fooled you right and tight. You never seen this morning coming."

I wanted to scream that she was wrong, but the presence of Caleb's backpack in Jake's shop put the lie to that. Could I be that wrong? Could I have raised such a monster?

"You're seeing it now, ain't you? All them little hints that mothers try to ignore. He's not your sweet little boy anymore. He's ours. He's an Everett through and through and there ain't no going back for him."

Whatever I would have said to her at that moment was lost when Caleb came stomping into the house with his father.

I stared at the two of them. Watched the same look of shock cross their faces, then the malicious grins that matched each other smirk for smirk.

"What the hell are you doing here?" asked Caleb. "You're supposed to be dead. We heard the explosion. Even saw that cool ball of fire blast out of the parking garage."

The pair of them high-fived. My brain kept screaming, "Two peas, two peas, two peas in a pod."

I stared at this small stranger, this despicable excuse for a human being, and wondered how I could have been so blind. "You're disappointed?"

"Of course I am. You're going to spoil everything."

"Spoil everything?"

"I want to live with my father. We've been planning this since last summer."

My brain felt numb. "Last summer?"

"Yeah, remember when I told you I'd found a friend to go

fishing with at the lake? Well, that was Dad. We've been talking and planning ever since."

"Was part of your plan to kill Jake?"

Caleb looked at his mirror image and the two of them giggled. "We knew he was the only one who'd raise a ruckus when I went missing. It was so easy. I distracted him while Dad came in behind him with the knife. Slit his throat like it was nothing but a stick of butter."

Any feelings I'd ever had for Caleb drained from my body. The child I had mothered for twelve years was gone. Vanished. There was nothing left for me to salvage. Nothing. I wanted to blame somebody, but there was nobody to blame but myself. Myself, and my fear of dying, or worse yet, being raped again. My fear had killed Jake.

I felt the gun in my pocket. There was only one solution but did I have the strength to make things right? I slid the gun from my pocket, pulled the trigger, and watched the mirror crack. I saw him fall to the floor and felt nothing.

I head Amos' voice in the back of my mind. "Watch your back, baby." The boy's father was making a grab for the shotgun and I pulled the trigger one more time. The mirror shattered and my fear with it.

A keening whine came from the old woman as she knelt down on the floor. She looked up at me and asked, "Why?"

"It needed doing."

• • •

I woke this morning in a strange hotel room and for the first time in years I'm not afraid of what the day will bring. I find myself in the strange position of being a murderer but the upside is that I'm no longer a victim. For better or worse I've taken my life back. I considered turning myself in but how could I make the police understand what happened when I barely understood myself?

The rape. The years of fear. The bank. The security guard.

The bomb. Jake. Caleb. I was no longer a law-abiding citizen, nor was I a single mother living a normal life. Perhaps I never had been. I have no idea what the future will bring but at least I can face it without constant fear.

Unexpectedly I found myself walking down the alley where Amos lived, back to the one place I'd felt safe through all this. He was sitting next to the dumpster with a vacant look on his face. I handed him a brown paper bag with the lip of a bottle sticking out. His eyes brightened as he reached for the bag.

Sliding down in the space beside him I said, "You were right. Violence does breed violence."

Amos squinted his eyes and peered at me. "Looks like you come out alright."

I laid my head on his chest. He put his arm around me and patted my shoulder. I could hear the sound of his heart beating a welcome to my weary soul and felt the first tears burn their way down my face.

"Hallelujah, and pass the green beans," shouted Amos before taking another swig from the bottle and passing it back to me.

"I'm fresh out of green beans. Would a ham sandwich do?" I asked.

A smile split is dirty face. "Better than green beans."

I don't know what life will bring my way, but then who does? Maybe time with Amos will help me figure that out. For now, home is this cluttered alley full of invisible people. And I'm happy to be one of them.

BRICK HOUSE

BY MICHAEL BAILEY

She ran her tongue across my teeth and at first I didn't know what to do, but then my body told me to open my mouth to taste the mint on her breath and to feel the wet warmth she offered me. Her smile got me to smile. I wasn't sure I wanted Erick Lock so close to my face, but that is how we ended up, only inches from one another. I remember smelling spearmint and blushing as she placed her hand on the back of my neck. Her amber eyes bounced right to left and left to right while I tried to keep up with them. She traced the edges of my lips with scarlet fingernails and I trembled. I brought my own hand to her cheek and connected her freckles with an imaginary line, feeling the single dimple at the corner of her mouth, the cat scratch scar on her chin, the soft skin of her neck and the pulse of our two hearts beating rhythmically together. It was partially fear and partially confusion, just emotions crashing oddly together as one: love.

Did I love her? We had only just met the summer before our sophomore year of college. Did I want her inches from my face? Did I want her looking into my eyes so lustfully? Did I want her to trace my lips with her fingers, to grab by neck, to lean into me with her body pressed ever so gently against my own?

I wasn't sure at the time, but it felt right somehow as she ran her tongue across my teeth, melting me deep into her arms as she wrapped them around me and I closed my eyes knowing she was still watching them to see what I would do, and then I leaned into her and opened my mouth slightly and let her in and tasted the mint as she fed it to me. Her hand got lost deep into my hair as blood rushed upward from my chest and downward to the rest of my body—losing my breath, losing my mind—and I couldn't breathe as she sucked the air from my lungs, and I couldn't breathe as my heart palpitated, and I couldn't breathe as she pulled away and took my heart and finally I opened my eyes to see Erica Lock, her eyes no longer dancing. She was trembling and I could feel her heart beating through her chest and through her breasts because they were pressed against me. She took in air between trembling lips. I touched them with the tip of a finger, moving to the dimple forming at the crescent of her smile. My other hand held the small of her back and I could feel the dampness of sweat. I remember feeling her hand in my hair and I wanted it to stay there forever. I didn't want the moment to end although only moments before I was unsure I even wanted it to begin. And then my mother walked in on us as we held each other tenderly on the bed.

It was an unexpected visit, to say the least. She wanted to see my dorm, to make sure I was doing fine on my own, to make sure I was eating right and keeping my room clean, to see if I was living up to the hype I relived to her through my letters back home. She didn't want to walk in on me holding a girl. She didn't want to see us kissing, but that didn't matter. I didn't date much in high school. I didn't go to Homecoming, Sadie Hawkins, Prom, or any other school dance. She didn't want me to date until I turned sixteen and after I turned sixteen I honestly wasn't ready to date. I was still searching for myself, and until I could find myself, I wasn't really sure I wanted to share it with anyone. My mother walked in on me masturbating once. I forgot to lock the door and was lying naked on my back on the bed, the sheet only a crumpled mess at my legs. It must have slid down while I was finding myself. I was in mid-orgasm when the door opened, my back arched into the air. The expression on her face changed from innocent to horror-stricken as my face changed from coital to horror-stricken. I fell back to the bed and pulled the sheets over my exposed body and yelled at her to get out while the spasms between my legs lessened and my heartbeats hastened. She gasped and slammed the door. I gasped just trying to catch my breath as I tried to rejoin my mind with my body and tried to forget my stupidity for not locking the door. Twice she had walked in on me unexpected. Twice she found me gasping for air at my most intimate of moments.

"Get your hands off my daughter," my mother said when she saw us together on the bed in my dorm room. Erica took her advice and took a lock of my hair with it; somehow, while caressing my neck, she had gotten some of my ponytail stuck in her ring.

This is the part of the story where some of you will be taken aback; flipping to reread the last few pages to make sure you didn't miss anything. Some sort of trick, perhaps. The only trick is that some of you simply assumed I was a young man and are now shocked to find me otherwise. Some of you will even stop reading and set this story aside, disgusted. Whether or not you accept it, the truth about me is simple: I have a second X chromosome; I have a vagina. There is no gimmick. Love is love. This is a love story. This is a tragedy. This is a story about two people becoming one and I don't expect you to like it. In fact, I don't want you to like it; I want you to hate it. I want you to feel saddened by the time you reach the end.

The young woman at my side hid her face and I tried to pull her hand away, but she turned toward the window. My mother pointed at her and said, "I won't have you turn my daughter into no lesbian." She said the word like a curse, like it was a bad thing for one woman to love another. It hurt to hear her say it like that. "Mom! Get out!" But she stayed. She sized me up from head to toe, disgusted, her upper lip curled. I had tainted the holy body she had given me by "experimenting" as she put it. I tried telling her I wasn't experimenting with anything. I was finding myself. I was finding love. I was finding a way to express the feelings deep down in my body that wanted out. They wanted Erica Lock. "Tess," she sighed, and that was all she wanted to say by the tone in her voice, my name, but then she said something that would make me hate her for the next few years. Four simple words: you're not my daughter. "What?" Both Erica and I said it at the same time. Erica turned to face me and then glared at my mother. I truly fell in love with her then. Our hands, clammy, bound us together as she scooted closer. I think it was then, as well, that Erica fell for me. "You're not my daughter," my mother repeated. A single tear fell from my left eye and ran along the bridge of my nose. I felt it drip and land on my blouse. "Because of this?" I asked, looking into a set of amber eyes. Erica looked down to our hands. "You don't love her," my mother said. "You don't understand love. I always knew there was something wrong with you. Your father and I both thought you might find out someday, but this, this fad, this faze, this whatever it is in your life, it should prove to you that you're not my daughter—" She cut herself short. She wouldn't even look at us. We disgusted her. "But Dad—" I started. "Your father is dead, Tess. He and your mother died shortly after you were born. We didn't want to tell you because we thought you might find out and do something drastic, like this…" I wanted to kiss Erica in front of her. I wanted to disgust her, then, by reaching my hands under Erica's shirt and pulling her toward me, by pulling her shirt over her head and pulling her toward me as our mouths connected and our tongues danced. But that would be unfair to Erica and deep down that's not what I wanted to do. I wanted to slap my… this woman across the face for belittling me, for disowning me so easily because of something as meager as fear. "And Katie?" I asked. "I gave birth to your sister, just not you. James, your adoptive father…" she kept rambling, but I had stopped listening. James had been my father for twenty plus years of my life; my mother…not my mother, she made him a stranger to me in only a moment; she had made herself a stranger. Because I kissed a girl, because she walked in on me as I was finding myself— twice now—and because I no longer fit her precious daughter mold, she had disowned me. Part of me didn't want to believe her. I rose from the bed and faced her. She took half a step back because I was nothing but a sick little girl to her. "Look at me," I said, and it took her a while, but she finally did. "I fucking hate you," I told her, just above a whisper. I made sure she was looking into my eyes so she knew I meant every word. Tears ran freely from my eyes. She was letting me go and I was letting her go. I let her slap me across the face and when she left I locked the door.

The relationship between my mother and me for the next few years remained mutually distant. We saw each other at Thanksgiving and Christmas, for my younger sister Katie's sake, perhaps, but our gatherings were usually silent except for the sounds of silverware scraping over my grandmother's china. Sometimes my father—I still call both my adoptive parents mother and father—would ask about my schooling and I'd tell him it was fine and say nothing more. During Katie's sixteenth birthday party I remember a conversation that came up about boys. Katie wasn't supposed to start dating until she turned sixteen, but she had been seeing this boy named Zach since she was fifteen and a half. When we were alone, Katie asked me what sex was like and I told her sex was like electricity, starting deep inside and riding up your spine. She admitted to having sex once, but it was nothing like electricity, that it hurt. I explained to her that it would eventually stop hurting and that she'd probably become addicted to it. "Mom won't go with me to get a prescription for birth control," she told me. I asked if she and Zach had used a condom and she said Zach had like a million of them in his sock drawer but, for the most part, what they did together didn't call for protection. "When did *you* start having sex?" she asked me. My first time was junior year in high school. Some jock named Joss Thompson. She asked if it hurt and I said yes, at first. She asked if it felt like electricity riding up my spine. It didn't. It felt like a five-minute violation of my body, but I didn't tell Katie that. I told her what she needed to be told, that love is an emotion, and without love, sex is just two people fucking. We laughed and then Mom and Dad walked around the corner and surprised us. "What's so funny?" asked Dad. "No secrets, you two." Katie told them we were discussing boys. Mom just stood there with a straight face.

"Boys, huh?" she said. Katie didn't know about Erica. Dad pretended someone had flagged him down and left the three of us. Outside, a mixture of adolescent boys and girls were throwing water balloons at one another. "You tell Katie you're seeing someone?" Katie let out a high-pitched noise and punched me on the shoulder. "What's his name—do I know him—is he cute?" she asked. "*Mom...*" I said and sighed. "Your sister's dying to know, Tess. Look, she's ecstatic." And she was. She was smiling, her eyes glossy from the kitchen's florescent lighting. "Electricity," she said and giggled. Mom was clueless. "Fine," I said. "Lock." Katie grabbed my arm and said, "Is there emotion, or are you two just, you know..." I did know, but Mom didn't know, so I told her: "Yes, there is love." My mother rolled her eyes and folded her arms disapprovingly. "Lock's just the last name," my mother said, and then, "Tell Katie the rest of *his* name." I looked right at my little sister and came out of my imaginary closet. "Erica Lock." The corner of my mother's lips curled up again. Katie gave a crooked smile and said innocently, "Erica Lock? But that's my friend Jennifer's older sister—oh." There was shock in her voice, but no disgust. "So you're... and she's..." I nodded, and then she asked me the question I expected her to ask. "And there's emotion, and electricity?" My mother had had enough. She stormed away and joined the party outside. My sister was the first person I ever told. She's the only one so far, besides Erica, to accept it. "It's like Nikola Tesla put a Jacob's ladder between my legs," I told her. "Cool," she said, and then, "Does my friend Jennifer know about her sister? I won't say anything." She knew. And then Katie asked me a few more questions about sex and boys and semen and we walked outside to have some fun on her birthday.

Erica and I stayed together until our senior year of college. I met her parents once. I was introduced to them as one of her girlfriends from school and they just assumed I was just another one of her friends. If we were both boys and I was instead introduced as one of her boyfriends, they may have thought of us differently. Our relationship was hidden. We'd hang out between classes, share lunches, go to the movies on the weekends and out to dinner, but we never shared anything physical with the public. Every once in a while we'd get to talking and one of us would brush the other's hand, but we usually caught ourselves and pulled back. Sometimes at the theatre when the lights dimmed we'd hold hands, but only if we were alone in the aisle. Sometimes it was difficult to hide our emotions simply because our emotions weren't socially accepted. One day Erica and I were sitting alone under the elm tree outside of the chemistry building finishing homework assignments when she said, "Let's do it." I remember looking up from my calculus book and saying, "I can't. I have volleyball practice in an hour and a monster history test tomorrow morning." She said, "No, not *it* it. Let's come out. Why should we hide the fact that we love each other?" Butterflies fluttered in my stomach and I felt I was going to float away, my face red from the heart beating madly in my chest. I was in love with Erica Lock, but had never told her, and it was the first time I heard her say that she loved me. I looked around nervously to see if anyone were watching—part of me didn't care anymore—before grabbing her hand within my own. "Do you want to?" I did, and I told her I did, and then I leaned forward to kiss her. Before our lips could make contact, jock Bobby Allison and his friend Trey walked by and Bobby said, "Trey, check it out." Erica and I both turned to find a finger pointing at us. "Nice…" said Trey. "Sick," said Bobby, but 'sick' had recently become synonymous for 'bitchin,' the same way 'bad' had changed meaning in the mid-eighties from something bad to something good. "Yeah," said Trey, "lesbians are so fucking hot." And then they were gone. Erica laughed and I laughed and we were both blushing because we were both out now, and with Bobby and Trey seeing what they saw, rumors of us having wild sex in public under the elm tree in front of the chemistry building would soon spread. The rumors indeed spread and soon it seemed as if the entire campus knew about us. People were constantly turning their heads. At the time, there were only a few outed individuals and only one other couple, but as the weeks turned to months, more and more students came out—to us, anyway. "I wish I had the nerve to come out," said a boy from my calculus class, and then, "You won't tell anyone, will you? It's just between us?" One girl from track came up to me one day and said, "If you ever need anyone to talk to…" and then she walked away. If I could put a number to it, I would say about a tenth of all the people I knew at school were gay, teachers included. I quickly learned all of their secrets.

Things were looking positive until the Saturday before graduation. Just down the street from the theatre was a small coffee shop called Cupa Joe; we were on our way to get some iced coffees when Erica said, "Isn't that your mom?" It was. She was walking out of a small bookstore called Hidden Passages, which was right next to the coffee shop. She held a book, but I couldn't make out the title because her purse was pressed against it as she fished for money to buy a coffee. "You want to go somewhere else?" asked Erica. Something inside me said we should try someplace else, but I was tired of hiding from my mother. We followed her inside and once we were in line I said casually, "Hey, Mom," as if we had just seen each other not too long ago. It had been close to six months since we last spoke, and it wasn't on good terms. She turned on her heels, looked at me, looked at Erica, looked at me again. "Hey, sweetie," she said before giving me a hug. I still couldn't read the title of the book. I had no idea why she felt the impulse to hug me, but it felt nice to feel that connection with her again. "Erica, right?" she said, and then gave Erica a hug, too. Well, half a hug. This wasn't my mother, yet somehow it was. I was surprised she even remembered her name. "Nice to see you again. Can I buy the two of you some coffee?" Erica and I shared confused expressions and we both half-smiled. Who was this woman? "Sure," I said, and then the three of us were ordering our drinks. When she paid the cashier she set the book on the counter face down and I could see the binding. The title was *My Girl Likes Girls*, or something similar. I can't quite remember the exact title because of the events that happened next, but it was something close to that and it was the first time my mother ever really tried understanding me. The book was a start, at least. It was cute. We got our drinks after waiting through an uneasy silence and my mother asked if we wanted to sit together at one of the tables outside. As we walked out the door, a noisy diesel truck roared down the street. I recognized it as belonging to one of the aggies that went to our college. Some called them hicks. I can still remember his face, but not his name, as if it were erased from my mind. There was another in the cabin, and three others crouched in the bed. I can still remember the hatred behind one of their voices that called out, "Goddamn dikes!" as the rusted truck raced by us.

The brick hit Erica across the bridge of her noise, diagonally from her left eye to her right cheekbone, and I will never forget the sound it made striking her. She fell immediately and I grabbed her hand and fell with her. She landed hard on the sidewalk, cracking the back of her head. My mother dropped her book and dropped her coffee and screamed, "Oh my God!" as she hid her own nose with her hands and stared at the mess they had made of Erica Lock. Blood instantly welled at the gash across her face and at the back of her head. What was left of the brick lay scattered around her body in a half dozen broken pieces. Erica still held onto her coffee cup as her eyes rolled back into her head and she convulsed. "Oh my God!" my mother screamed again. I grabbed the back of Erica's head and placed a hand across the wound and felt pieces of cheekbone shift under my fingertips as I tried to hold in the red that so eagerly wanted out of her. She sputtered as she tried to talk but after a moment she was silent, her body still. I looked to her chest and found that she had stopped breathing. Her pulse slowed and soon I could no longer feel it beating against my skin. My mother was silent. She found no god to take her away from the horror. The book she had purchased to help her understand her adopted daughter lay open, the life of my love pooling around it and soaking into its pages. She knelt down next to me and removed her scarf and held it against the back of Erica's head as she screamed for someone to call an ambulance while the tears rolled down her face. She tried to hold Erica together while I performed CPR. I switched back and forth from compressions to respirations, wondering what my mother thought of me as I put my lips to Erica's so she could breathe me in. It was the first time I ever kissed her in public, in front of my mother, in front of anyone, but no one seemed to mind. She tasted like spearmint and all I could think about was our first kiss, our faces inches from one another, the trembling, our pulses beating together rhythmically, and then Erica opened her eyes and gasped for air, her back arching slightly. One of her eyes was swollen shut, but the other bounced right to left and left to right as I tried to keep up with it. She reached up with a shaky hand and traced my lips and then ran her fingers through my hair and through all of her confusion and pain I could make out the beginning of a dimple at the corner of her mouth as she tried to smile. As her hand fell back to her side I noticed some of my hair was stuck in her ring. She closed her eyes and died.

THE CONTRIBUTORS

Michael Bailey is the multi-award-winning author of PALINDROME HANNAH, PHOENIX ROSE and PSYCHOTROPIC DRAGON (novels), SCALES AND PETALS and INKBLOTS AND BLOOD SPOTS (short story / poetry collections), and editor of PELLUCID LUNACY and the CHIRAL MAD anthologies.

John Boden lives a stones throw from Three Mile Island with his wonderful wife and sons. A baker by day, he spends his off time writing or working on Shock Totem. His work has appeared in 52 STITCHES, BLACK INK HORROR, WEIRDYEAR, NECON E-BOOKS, SHOCK TOTEM, the John Skipp edited PSYCHOS and a few upcoming projects. His not-really-for-children children's book, DOMINOES is a pretty cool thing.

Kealan Patrick Burke is the Bram Stoker Award-winning author of five novels, six collections, and over a hundred short stories. A movie based on his story "Peekers" is currently in development at Lionsgate Entertainment. Visit him on the web at www.kealanpatrickburke.com

MP Johnson's short stories have appeared in more than 40 publications. His debut book, THE AFTER LIFE STORY OF PORK KNUCKLES MALONE, was released by Bizarro Pulp Press. His second book, DUNGEONS AND DRAG QUEEENS, is out now from Eraserhead Press. He is the creator of Freak Tension zine, a B-movie extra and an obsessive music fan currently based in Minneapolis.

Ed Kurtz is the author of A WIND OF KNIVES, THE FORTY-TWO, and ANGEL OF THE ABYSS. His short fiction has appeared in Thuglit, Needle, Shotgun Honey, Beat to a Pulp, Out of the Gutter, and numerous anthologies. Ed lives in Texas where he is at work on his next project. Visit him online at www.edkurtz.net.

Lucas Mangum writes horror, crime and fantasy fiction, sometimes horrific crime fantasies. His work has appeared on the websites Shotgun Honey and MicroHorror as well as the anthologies Strange World, crappy shorts-deuces wild, and Bones. His novel, FLESH AND FIRE, is due out in 2015 as part of Journalstone Publishing's Double Down Series. Blog at lucasmangumauthor. com, Twitter @LMangumFiction, and Facebook at facebook.com/lucas.mangum

Nick Medina is an author from Chicago, Illinois. He has been published in print, online and audio formats by magazines, journals and anthologies in the United States and the United Kingdom. To contact Nick, or to read more of his work, visit http://nickjmedina.wix.com/nickmedina or follow him on Twitter: @ MedinaNick.

Sandra Seamans is a short story writer whose work has appeared in a variety of anthologies and zines, both print and online. You can learn more about her and short stories at *My Little Corner* (http://sandraseamans.blogspot.com/)

Jessie Volk has published several scientific articles as a research scientist in San Francisco, but this is her first work of fiction. When she's not writing or working, she can be found meditating or practicing Goju Ryu Karate in a dojo on the edge of Golden Gate Park. Jessie lives with her husband and two cats in a tiny apartment nowhere near as strange as her story setting. She is not afraid of the dark.

Jonathan Woodrow writes dark, mostly speculative fiction. His work has appeared in various publications, including the July 2013 issue of Under the Bed Magazine, the November, 2013 issue of Roar and Thunder Magazine, and most recently, his nauseating short story Candy Stain will be included in the upcoming anthology, Cranial Leakage, published by Grinning Skull Press.

Bracken MacLeod lives in New England and has worked as a martial arts teacher, a university philosophy instructor, for a children's non-profit, and as a criminal and civil trial attorney. While he tries to avoid using the law education, he occasionally finds uses for the martial arts and philosophy training. His stories have appeared in Sex and Murder Magazine, Every Day Fiction, Femme Fatale: Erotic Tales of Dangerous Women, Reloaded: Both Barrels Vol. 2, and Ominous Realities from Gray Matter Press. His debut novel, MOUNTAIN HOME, is available from Books of the Dead Press on Amazon and Barnes and Noble, and his novella, WHITE KNIGHT, is available from One Eye Press.

Jan Kozlowski is a freelance writer, editor and researcher. Her first novel DIE, YOU BASTARD! DIE! was published in 2012 by John Skipp's Ravenous Shadows imprint. Her short stories have appeared in HUNGRY FOR YOUR LOVE: An Anthology of Zombie Romance and FANGBANGERS: An Erotic Anthology of Fangs, Claws, Sex and Love, both edited by Lori Perkins, and in NECON EBOOKS FLASH FICTION ANTHOLOGY BEST OF 2011. You can visit her at JanKozlowski.com.

Ron Earl Phillips lives nestled in the foothills of West Virginia with his wife, daughter and one too many cats. He is the publisher and managing editor of One Eye Press, and is responsible for Shotgun Honey (Crime), The Big Adios (Western), and Blight Digest (Horror). He has been known to write. Find out more at RonEarlPhillips.com.

THANK YOU FOR READING

Fall 2014   DIGEST

PLEASE VISIT US ONLINE

WWW.BLIGHTDIGEST.COM